SANDRA BROWN

TEMPEST IN EDEN

WARNER BOOKS

NEW YORK   BOSTON

Copyright © 1983 by Sandra Brown
All rights reserved. No part of this book may be reproduced in any form or by any electronic or mechanical means, including information storage and retrieval systems, without permission in writing from the publisher, except by a reviewer who may quote brief passages in a review.

This Warner Books edition is published by arrangement with the author.

Warner Books

Time Warner Book Group
1271 Avenue of the Americas, New York, NY 10020
Visit our Web site at www.twbookmark.com

Printed in the United States of America

First Warner Books Printing: March 1996
Reissued: May 2001, April 2005

10 9 8 7 6 5 4 3 2 1

ISBN 978-0-446-61681-2   ISBN 0-446-61681-8

By Sandra Brown

Dear Reader,

For years before I began writing general fiction, I wrote genre romances under several pseudonyms. *Tempest in Eden* was originally published more than ten years ago (under my first pen name, Rachel Ryan).

This story reflects the trends and attitudes that were popular at the time, but its themes are eternal and universal. As in all romance fiction, the plot revolves around star-crossed lovers. There are moments of passion, anguish, and tenderness—all integral facets of falling in love.

I very much enjoyed writing romances. They're optimistic in orientation and have a charm unique to any other form of fiction. If this is your first taste of it, please enjoy.

Sandra Brown

TEMPEST
IN EDEN

Chapter One

"This is a cabin in the woods?" Shay Morrison muttered to herself as she slowed her compact car to a halt in front of a two-story dwelling. Situated atop a gentle rise, the structure had a rough timber exterior but was otherwise far from rustic.

Shay pushed open the car door and got out, regarding the acreage surrounding the house with appreciation. Virginally green with the first buds of summer, the forested landscape was breathtaking. At least her mother hadn't exaggerated about that.

Shay smiled, remembering the conversations with her mother just two days before. "But, Shay, you must come. He's dying to meet you."

"And I'm dying to meet the man who hustled you to the altar," Shay had said. She hadn't been notified of her mother's marriage until after the fact and couldn't keep from ribbing her mother for marrying so hastily after having been a widow for seven years. "What was the rush? You aren't pregnant, are you?"

She heard her mother's familiar, resigned sigh. "Shame on you, Shay. When will you learn to speak like a lady?"

"When *not* being one stops being so much fun." She had laughed lightly.

"I know I should have told you about the wedding, but . . . well, everything happened so fast. There we were sitting in John's son's house, sipping coffee, and the next minute we were reciting the vows." Her mother sighed blissfully in remembrance. "We made up our minds and acted on the decision immediately. It was so romantic."

"I'm sure it was, and I'm glad for you," Shay said sincerely.

"You will join us this weekend, won't you? John is so looking forward to meeting you."

Shay nervously twisted the telephone cord. It wasn't that she really minded her mother marrying again. Celia Morrison had been alone too long. After having been happily married to Shay's father for twenty-seven years, his death had been a hard blow. John Douglas had been described to Shay as a retired businessman who was interesting, fun, handsome, and deliriously in love with her mother. Of course, that had been her mother's assessment.

"I don't know, Mother. You're barely out of the honeymoon stage and—"

"Don't be ridiculous. We really do want you to spend the weekend with us or else we wouldn't have invited you. Please, Shay. It's very important to me to unite my new family."

A weekend in a cabin sounded a bit lame to someone with Shay's zest for life, but she supposed she could make this one concession to her only parent. It might not be full of fun, but she could get some well-earned rest. "Where and when?" she asked.

"Oh, how marvelous," Celia cried enthusiastically. She gave Shay directions to the cabin near Kent Falls in western Connecticut. Shay insisted she drive her own car rather than take the train. She didn't want to have to rely on train schedules to make a speedy escape should the boredom of the weekend induce her to leave before Sunday afternoon.

"The countryside is lovely. Wait until you see the cabin," Celia gushed.

Shay glanced at her watch and realized she would be late for a sitting if she didn't hurry. "I'll be there sometime Friday evening if I can get off work Saturday. That's customarily a busy day at the gallery."

"I'm sure you can arrange it if you explain the circumstances to Mr. Vandiveer. We'll have such fun. I can't wait for you to meet Ian."

"Ian?" Oh, please, no, Shay groaned to herself. "The son?"

"Why, of course. This is the joining of two families, remember?"

Terrific. A whole weekend in a remote cabin in the woods with an older couple acting like silly adolescents in the throes of first love and a new stepbrother who probably wouldn't be any more enthusiastic about the arrangement than she was. "I've got to go, Mom. I'm posing for a photographer this afternoon."

"An artist?"

"No. Very commercial this time. Legs only. An ad for a lady's razor."

"Oh."

Celia kept it no secret that she sometimes felt uneasy about her daughter's profession. Before she could launch into an interrogation, Shay said, "I'll see you Friday. Bye, Mom."

Now Friday afternoon found Shay climbing up the wooden steps to the wide front porch of the cabin, a weekend hideaway belonging to her mother's new husband. The legs that had been photographed *au naturel* only a few days before were now encased in tight-fitting jeans that molded to her figure. They hugged her shapely calves and enhanced the length and form of her thighs.

The front door of the house had a note tacked to it: *"Go on in. John and I buying groceries. Back soon."*

Shay was surprised when she tested the doorknob and found it unlocked. Apparently there were still places in rural America where people felt at ease about leaving their houses unsecured.

The door opened onto a room that ran the width of the house. Cozy and homey, it offered several couches and chairs to curl up in, a stone fireplace, uncovered windows with a panoramic view, throw rugs on a polished oak floor, vases of fresh flowers placed strategically on tables and shelves, and countless books and records stored in floor-to-ceiling shelves. Shay was impressed as she closed the door behind her.

Making a cursory inspection of the lower floor, she saw a friendly kitchen that was thoroughly modern but quaint in design, a dining room with a long maple table and captain's chairs, and a storage pantry with a washing machine and dryer.

"John doesn't believe in roughing it," she said to herself as she returned to the living room and climbed the stairs to the second story. Directly in front of her as she stepped onto the landing was a wide window with a spectacular view of the gently rolling countryside. On either side of the stairs were doors leading to bedrooms. Another note almost exactly like the one on the front door was tacked to one of these: *"Shay's room."*

"Mother thinks of everything." Pushing open the door to the bedroom, she got only a flashing first glance at the brass headboard with white porcelain knobs, the apple-green quilted comforter over the white eyelet dust ruffle, the white wicker rocking chair, and the cheery lace curtains at two windows before she was brought to attention by loud singing coming from an adjoining bathroom.

The masculine voice was singing an innovative rendition of a Beach Boys song. Shay laughed out loud. The voice was singing all the parts from the lowest bass to the highest falsetto. Every once in a while he threw in a *ba-da-da-da* to simulate drums. He was accompanied by the pulsing rhythm of the shower's spray.

"Hello," Shay called out, wanting to alert the shower-taker that he wasn't alone and that he had left the door to her bedroom open. The song continued even as the water was shut off. Shay heard the click of the shower door being swung wide. She opened her mouth to speak again, but no words passed her lips. She stared in speechless awe as a long, muscled leg extended out of the shower stall. A foot, well-shaped with a high arch, groped for the bath mat before standing firmly on it. A lean body followed the foot. A sinewy arm and a hand that conveyed both sensitivity and strength dragged a towel from the bar on the shower door.

Shay rushed across the room, intending to shut the door before the man saw her. He was now singing into the towel as he vigorously rubbed his head with it. Momentarily, almost involuntarily, she indulged herself in a view of the naked male form in all its splendor.

Wide shoulders and chest tapered to a slender waist and narrow hips. Water ran down the magnificent torso in crystal rivulets that called attention to the texture and hue of his tanned skin. Droplets beaded on dark, curling hair that matted the deep chest and halved the flat stomach with a ribbon of black satin. The muscles of his back rippled smoothly as he moved. His legs were bunched with hard, sleek muscles. Taut buttocks tightened as he leaned forward over the basin to peer at his reflection in the mirror. He slung the towel haphazardly around his neck and ran slender fingers through his mop of wet black hair.

Then he saw her reflection in the mirror. Her expression was rapt, her lips slightly parted, her brown eyes wide with admiration.

"What—" He spun around as though he had seen a ghost and needed desperately to assure himself that it wasn't really there.

Dazzling blue eyes speared into Shay, and she wondered in some detached part of her mind if his black lashes looked spiky and thick because they were still wet or if they were like that all the time.

Incredulity, embarrassment, shock, and dismay were all stamped on the man's rugged features. His face looked like the embodiment of masculine perfection that some talented sculptor had decided to have fun with. After arranging the features perfectly, the witty artist had carved absolute disbelief onto them. The result was comical.

Shay responded befittingly. She laughed. "Hi," she said cheekily, "I'm Shay Morrison." She extended her hand, barely maintaining her composure, somehow keeping from collapsing into unrestrained hysteria at the ludicrousness of the situation.

He looked at her hand stupidly, as though he'd never seen one before. Then his blue eyes, still disbelieving, swung back to her face. He whipped the towel from around his neck. Shay had the distinct notion that he didn't know whether to cover his face, as would a guilty child, or to cover the part of him that undeniably declared his sex. He opted for the latter and wrapped the towel clumsily around his waist, holding it precariously as he said tersely, "Ian Douglas."

"John's son! My new stepbrother!" Shay chortled, finally giving in to the laughter that was building within her chest. "It's so . . . so nice . . . to meet you," she said between bursts of hilarity.

Irritation thinned his wide, full lips. "If you'll excuse me, Miss Shay." He reached for the door and began to close it.

Through the narrowing crack she called, "I'll see you later, Ian. Not as much of you, of course." The door slammed shut in her face. Turning away from it, she laughed all the harder. Imagine her meeting her new stepbrother in such a fashion.

She trooped down the stairs to retrieve her bags from the car. She had traveled light, bringing only casual clothes. Her mother had stressed that they wouldn't be going into town, but staying at the cabin all weekend. As she made her way back up the stairs, she heard dishes rattling in the kitchen. Ian Douglas must be dressed and downstairs.

She deposited her bags on the floor beside the bed, deciding to unpack later. Checking herself in the mirror, she saw that her hair could stand a brushing. Its wheat-colored strands hung to her shoulders. The natural curliness that she had cursed as a child she was now thankful for. Her hair was often an asset in her work, adding a wildness, a hint of the primitive to her "look," which artists and photographers often found intriguing. The dark chocolate color of her eyes made her even more exotic. After whisking a lip-glossing wand over her mouth, she straightened her short-sleeved red T-shirt and descended the stairs, anticipating her next encounter with the black-haired man who was her mother's stepson.

She found him glaring at a coffeemaker whose slow dripping, she gathered, was taxing his patience. When she entered the sunlit kitchen, he glanced at her

over his shoulder, then turned back to stare at the coffeemaker without acknowledging her presence.

His indifference galled her. For reasons she
couldn't name, she found it intolerable. She knew
men often found her attractive, though it rarely mat-
tered to her if they did or didn't. He may be her new
stepbrother, but he was a living, breathing male, and
it was suddenly paramount to her that he see her as
a female. Determination and pique tilted her chin ar-
rogantly.

"You've no reason to sulk. I called out a hello, you
know," she began defensively.

"Obviously not loud enough."

His unaccountable modesty puzzled her. Such shy-
ness over one's body had never been attributed to her,
but then considering her work, it wouldn't be. Perhaps
she went too far the other way, but this kind of modesty seemed disproportionate. Mr. Douglas must have
some real hang-ups, she decided.

Dressed, he was as attractive as undressed. His
speaking voice was as soothingly melodic as the vibrating tones of a stringed instrument in a master's
hands. It bothered her more than she cared to admit
that he seemed impervious to her as a woman, and she
was determined to get a reaction out of him. "If you
hadn't been screeching at the top of your lungs, you
would have heard me," she said.

"I was singing in the shower. A common practice, I believe."

"I didn't open the door to the bathroom; it was already opened. That was negligence on your part. Didn't you know I was expected? By the time I reached the door, you were stepping out of the shower with that towel around your head. What was I supposed to do?"

He turned to her then, and she was struck by his height. He towered over her a good six inches, though her willowy figure was considered tall for a woman. He had dressed in casual slacks and an open-collared sport skirt. The sleeves were rolled to his elbows, revealing the corded muscles of his forearms.

"Yes, Celia told me you were coming, but she said you wouldn't be here until later this evening. And as for what you could have done to prevent both of us from being embarrassed, you could have left the room immediately instead of standing there like a voyeur at a peep show."

Shay was delighted as he lowered his dark, shaggy brows over his luminescent eyes, revealing his anger. "*I* wasn't embarrassed," she said simply.

"You should have been."

"Why? Are you ashamed of your body? Do you think the human form is something dirty and shameful?"

He ground his startlingly white teeth together. "No."

"Then if it's not nakedness that upset you, it must have been me. Don't you like women?"

She flashed him a gamine smile and dropped into a chair. Bracing the heels of her hands on the seat between her knees, she leaned forward inquiringly. She knew the position was provocative. It pushed her breasts, unrestrained under the T-shirt, together to form a deep cleft between them. The cotton shirt wasn't sheer, but it conformed to her shape, leaving little to the imagination. In retrospect, she might be ashamed of herself, but at the moment a demonic sense of humor prompted her to goad his temper, which she knew lay very close to the surface.

With seeming disinterest, he turned to the cupboard and took down a coffee mug. "I like some women," he stated with an emphasis on *some.*

Trying to squelch her own rising temper, she snapped, "Just not the honest, independent, free-thinking ones. I can well imagine the type you like— meek and submissive." She rose from the chair and stalked angrily around the kitchen. She was angry at him for his indifference, and at herself for caring about it.

"Look, I said I was sorry," she said impatiently. "I don't know why you're making a federal case out of this. I saw you naked. So? If you'd had the chance, you'd have taken a good long look at me or any other woman, and don't even try to deny it. And your mind would have flown to thoughts much more intimate than mine."

"I haven't been intimate with any woman but my wife."

"You're married?" she asked, looking around in surprise, thinking she might see a ladylike, long-suffering, insipid creature materialize. Strange. She hadn't even considered the possibility that he might have a wife. She was sure her mother hadn't mentioned one.

"I was married."

"Divorced?" she asked.

"No. My wife's dead."

Her desire to provoke him took one last gasping breath and died. Her teasing smile faded into a shattered, pale expression of deep embarrassment and remorse. Slowly she sat back down in the chair. Unseeingly she stared through the screened back door. A nondescript station wagon was parked just beyond the porch. It hadn't been visible from the front of the house where she'd parked.

"I'm sorry," she said quietly. The only noise in the room was the gurgle of steaming coffee as he poured it into a mug. "Mom didn't tell me anything about you. I didn't know."

"Sugar?"

Her head came up to meet his stunning blue eyes. "Pardon?"

"Sugar. For your coffee."

"Oh, no . . . no. But cream or milk, please," she said, taking the mug from his outstretched hand. He went to the refrigerator and removed a carton of half-and-half, which he set on the table within her reach. "Thank you."

"You're welcome," he said formally, pouring himself some coffee. He took a seat across the table. For long moments he said nothing, only stared at the landscape through the windows and blew gently on his coffee to cool it before taking hesitant sips. At last he said quietly, "A drunk driver ran into us broadside one night. She was killed instantly. I walked away without a scratch. It's been almost two years. Better to tell people straight out. It saves them from asking and spares me having to answer."

Again a heavy silence ensued. Shay's love of life and everything in it was offended by such a waste of a valued human being. Her heart went out to the man who had suffered a senseless loss. She felt compelled to let him know she wasn't a stranger to heartache. "I was married, but it ended in divorce," she said thoughtfully. "Now we're a statistic. One of the thousands."

"As is Mary."

"Yes." Shay drank her coffee slowly. Covertly she

eyed him over the rim of her mug. In profile, his features looked more stern then they did face on. Perhaps it was the brilliance of his eyes that relieved some of the rigidity of his jaw and chin. Were those eyes what had compelled her to mention her unfortunate marriage? She never talked about the episode in her life to anyone. It was a closed subject. She had erased the memory, if not the pain, had even gone back to using her maiden name. Yet she had spoken of it to Ian Douglas. Why should a man she had just met inspire such confidence?

"Where do you live?" he asked at last, as if to fill the silent void.

"In Woodville, near Greenwich. It's small. Mostly commuters to New York live there."

"What do you do?"

His eyes were incredibly blue, and she found it hard to keep her mind on the subject. "Do?" she repeated, distracted. The doltish vagueness in her voice yanked her back into the present. "Do? Oh, I work in a gallery. We carry inexpensive works of art, decorating items, things like that."

"In Manhattan?"

"No, in Woodville. When I have to go to the city, I drive to Greenwich and take the train. But that's only once or twice a week."

"Once or twice a week? What takes you to New York once or twice a week?"

"I—"

She was cut off by the loud blaring of an automobile horn. They turned simultaneously to see a Mercedes sedan coming to a stop beside Ian's station wagon. As Shay watched, a silver-haired man got out of the driver's side, came around to the passenger side, and offered his hand to Celia. Her mother smiled happily as she took her husband's hand. He planted a soft kiss on her mouth before ushering her toward the back door.

Ian was there to greet them, holding the screen door open. "I thought my hostess and host had abandoned me," he said, slapping his father on the back. "Hi, Dad. Celia," he said more gently, leaning down to kiss her proffered cheek.

"Sorry we're so late getting back. Celia had an extensive grocery list. I hope you're hungry." John Douglas's eyes swept the room until they lighted on Shay. "Hello. You must be Shay."

"Darling, I'm so glad you came." Her mother extricated herself from John's arms and hurried to embrace her daughter. "How are you?"

"Fine," Shay said into her mother's soft, carefully coiffed brown hair. She hugged her gently and gazed down into a face that reflected deep joy. Smiling broadly, she said, "I don't need to ask how you are. You're positively radiant."

"And all because of John," her mother said in the

soft voice of an enthralled young girl. Stretching out her hand to clasp his, she pulled him forward. "John, this is my daughter Shay."

With no compunction, he took both her hands in his and let his eyes, a disturbingly familiar blue, roam freely over her face. "Shay, you're as beautiful as your mother." He kissed her on the cheek. "Forgive an aging man his impatience, but I was so eager to give my name to your mother, I wouldn't allow her the time to organize a formal wedding."

Shay smiled warmly at him. "You've made her very happy. I'd rather be a witness to that than the exchanging of vows."

"She's brought me more happiness than I ever thought to know again. You're welcome in our home anytime."

"Thank you."

He squeezed her hands once more before releasing them and turning toward Ian. "I see that you've met my son."

"Yes," Shay said, her eyes dancing with reawakened mischief. "I already feel like I know him very well."

"I'm so glad," Celia gushed. "John and I wanted the two of you to become close friends."

"You'd be amazed at how close I feel to him," Shay replied meaningfully. Her mother glanced at her warily, and Shay was immediately contrite. She knew that her impish grin and salty tone alerted Celia that she was up to something. Having seen first hand the happiness this marriage had brought her mother, she didn't want to do anything to spoil it. Putting her devious bent aside, she said humbly, "Ian and I were having a nice getting-acquainted discussion when you drove up."

"Yes," Ian said. After a significant pause he added, "We were discussing how one's conscience *should* be one's guide."

"Oh!" Shay choked on her coffee in startled outrage, her head coming up with a snap. She glared at him. "My conscience isn't one bit offended."

"Then maybe you should examine your morals."

"Ian . . ." John Douglas began uneasily.

"Oh, dear," said Celia. "And I was so hoping—"

"My morals are in great shape," Shay retorted, tilting her head back to look directly into Ian's face.

"You couldn't prove it by me."

"I don't need to prove anything to you," she snapped. She barely heard her mother's plea to calm herself. "I've never put much merit in the narrow-minded, pious, petty opinions of self-righteous prigs like you." Her breasts heaved with anger as she stared up into his chiseled face, gone hard with rage. "Excuse me," Shay said, moving swiftly toward the door. "I'm going to shower and change before dinner."

She stomped up the stairs and ran the coldest water

she could stand. But, rather than calming her, the shower fueled her agitation. "What a boor," she muttered as she dressed in a swirling skirt and peasant blouse of printed muslin. The soft, sheer fabric felt good against her skin as she lifted her arms to sweep her hair into a careless topknot. She let several curling tendrils lie with beguiling negligence on her neck and cheeks.

Ian Douglas represented everything she disdained. He was judgmental, stodgy, unyielding in what he considered to be the rules of propriety. He looked upon people like her with stern disapproval for their liberated outlook on life.

After nearly thirty years, she couldn't change herself, nor did she want to. Her father had been the only one who'd ever understood her. He alone had encouraged her independent nature, her liberal tolerance, her freethinking, her mischievous personality. When he had died, she'd lost not only a loving parent, but also her closest friend and staunchest ally.

She missed him still. He had been a physician, a man admired by his patients and constituents, adored and pampered by his wife, and loved by his daughter. They had shared a rare relationship, open and honest. While her mother had always been reluctant to discuss certain aspects of life with her daughter, Shay's father had always gone to great lengths to answer her every precocious question in detail. He had found her curiosity refreshing and entertaining, and had admired and encouraged her acceptance of other people, no matter what their lifestyles or philosophies. To those who had criticized her sometimes unorthodox behavior, he had defended her as being forthright and unpretentious.

Above all, Shay hated narrow-mindedness and those who would impose their brand of stuffy, stodgy, supercilious prudery on others. She tagged Ian Douglas as one of that breed. She only wished he looked more the part he played: with a nose that seemed perpetually turned up in distaste, myopic eyes that searched out indiscretions, and a pointed chin. Somehow it was hard to hate a flawless body that defined masculinity and a face that would have made Narcissus weep with envy.

It suddenly struck her that she was being unusually harsh and judgmental herself, jumping to conclusions about a man she'd only just met, but she pushed the thought aside impatiently.

"To hell with him," she said flippantly as she doused herself with a seductive scent. "I didn't ask for his opinion. I don't care what he thinks of me. Once this weekend is over, I don't ever have to see him again."

With that attitude, she descended the stairs. John and Ian were sitting in easy chairs, sipping chilled white wine from tulip-shaped glasses. "Shay," John called out, standing up, "come join us for a glass of wine."

She beamed at him and ignored his scowling son. "No thank you, John. I'm sure Mom can use my help in the kitchen." With a saucy swirl of her skirt, she pushed through the swinging door.

"What can I do?" she asked cheerfully. Her mother was bending down to pull a heavy casserole from the oven.

Her cheeks flushed becomingly from the heat of the stove, Celia turned around and sighed with despair. "You can march right upstairs and put on a bra, that's what you can do." Hands on hips, wearing a ruffled bibbed apron, her hair mussed, Celia Douglas looked anything but commanding.

"Why?" Shay asked breezily, going to the relish tray and popping an olive into her mouth.

Celia sputtered her answer. "Because . . . because I can see your . . . dew drops."

Shay nearly sucked the olive down her throat as she gasped a laugh. *"Dew drops?"* When she caught her breath, her eyes were dancing with mirth. "They're called nipples, mother. Nipples. And every woman since Eve has had them. They're part of the female anatomy. God created them. They're nothing to be ashamed of."

"They're nothing to flaunt either," Celia said with another weary sigh, conceding the argument, as she always did, to her daughter's winning pragmatism. "What will John and Ian think of you?"

Shay's grin melted, and she frowned. She went to the window and looked out at the lovely twilight-washed landscape. Unwittingly her mother had disarmed her in the most effective way. Shay was reminded of divided loyalties, personality conflicts, and failures to please. In her entire life, had she made anyone proud of her? "Are you ashamed of me, Mother?" she asked quietly.

"Oh, Shay," her mother said with instant remorse. "Of course not, darling." She came to her daughter quickly and placed a slender arm around her waist. "It's just that I wanted this to be a fun weekend with as little tension as possible. You've already had a run-in with Ian. By the way, what happened?"

"Nothing much. Just an instant, total, and unalterable dislike for each other." Shay saw no reason to explain the episode that afternoon any further.

"And you certainly didn't keep your aversion to yourself." Sighing, her mother released her and continued getting the dinner ready for serving. "When will you learn some decorum, Shay? I told your father he was courting disaster when he exercised no restraint in letting you see and hear things that a properly brought-up young lady should never be exposed to. He was far too liberal in his thinking, and it rubbed off on you."

"And I thank God for it," she said heatedly. When she saw her mother's anxious expression, she softened. "The dinner looks lovely, Mother. Your chicken paprika, if my nose doesn't deceive me." Taking up a tray to carry into the candlelit dining room, she added, "I'll try not to disgrace you in front of your new husband and stepson, Mom."

Celia's dinner did her proud. She had a knack that made stoneware and stainless look like priceless china and silver. She had arranged spring flowers in a crystal bowl for the centerpiece. Her cooking was unsurpassed. The years she had lived alone in widowhood had deprived her of the opportunity to use her homemaking talents. Now she was again in her element. Shay winked at her with a proud smile.

They commenced eating after John had asked Ian to say grace. Had it not been for Ian's deprecating glances across the linen tablecloth, Shay would have enjoyed the dinner immensely. John was a gentleman in every sense of the word, bridging the infrequent lapses in conversation with new topics of discussion.

"Your mother tells me you work in a gallery part-time, Shay," he said politely.

"Yes." She blotted her mouth with a napkin and pushed aside what little remained of her strawberry shortcake. "We cater to clients with excellent taste but limited budgets. For someone with a discerning eye, we carry an appreciable number of artworks."

"You must know quite a bit about art, then," John said, lighting an aromatic cigar with one of the candles.

"I should." Shay laughed. "I spend a great deal of time in art studios with artists."

"Oh? In what capacity?"

"She's worked for some of the best," Celia inserted nervously. "She's . . . They say no one else . . . Her . . ."

Shay's eyes slid across the table to Ian, who was sitting with his chin propped on his fist. His elbows rested on the arms of his chair. Candlelight gleamed on his black hair, which seemed perpetually tousled. He was staring into space with vacant blue eyes, apparently bored with the conversation.

Tossing her head defiantly, Shay determined to rout him out of his insouciance. "What my mother is tiptoeing around so timidly is that I'm a model. A highly specialized model." She paused dramatically. "I pose nude."

She turned toward the handsome man who was glowering at her with stern disapproval and countered his expression with one of smug triumph, knowing that the revelation would rattle him to the foundation of his bigoted soul.

But he met her dark eyes without flinching. His lips barely moved as he said softly, "And I'm a minister."

Chapter Two

For several stunned seconds Shay stared at Ian. Tearing her eyes from his at last, she looked to her mother for verification.

"I . . . I thought I mentioned that it was Ian who married us," Celia said in a soft whisper.

Acute embarrassment made Shay's cheeks burn with hot color. A dull roaring filled her eardrums, yet her mother's voice had the magnified, distorted pitch of someone speaking in a dream. "No," Shay croaked. "No, you didn't mention that Ian was a minister."

What had she said to this man? What had she done? Damn! He didn't look like any clergyman she'd ever seen. He didn't wear a Roman collar or robes or any of the solemn trappings she associated with the ministry. It wasn't fair that he sneaked around like a normal person, incognito, waiting to catch someone red-handed in a transgression.

Her embarrassment began to change to simmering anger for his not telling her about himself. He'd made a fool of her, and that stung her pride. But lashing out at him would only distress her mother. Instead Shay put on her most ingratiating smile, faced him, and said sweetly, "I hope my part-time occupation doesn't shock you, Reverend Douglas."

He took a sip of coffee nonchalantly. "Nothing you do would shock me."

She heard the undercurrent of scorn in his voice and pressed her lips into a thin line. Before she could offer a comeback, her mother intervened.

"I don't want either of you to get the wrong idea about what Shay does. She doesn't pose for men's magazines or anything like that." Celia laughed nervously.

"I don't need you to defend me to him," Shay said, aiming her ire exclusively at Ian.

"I'm not, Shay darling," her mother replied diplomatically. "I'm only trying to explain your work." Turning to face her husband, she added, "Shay's used by the most renowned artists, photographers, painters, and sculptors. She's the subject of works of art. Nothing she's posed for could ever be considered lewd."

Shay despised the pleading sound in her mother's voice. "Oh, for heaven's sake," she said in agitation, and pushed her chair away from the table with a scraping sound. "I'll do the dishes while the three of you hold a prayer meeting over my lost soul." Without another word, she flounced into the kitchen.

Minutes later, her arms were deep in hot, soapy water, a kitchen towel tucked into the waistband of her skirt in lieu of an apron. She didn't turn around when the door swung open behind her. Resolutely she continued with her task of scrubbing the cooking pots. She didn't want to talk to her mother just now. But her back stiffened with surprise when she heard an unmistakable low voice behind her.

"Do you want me to relieve you?"

"No," she answered curtly, striving to ignore the sudden pounding of her heart. "Why didn't your father install a dishwasher when he was building this place?" she asked crossly to cover her sudden nervousness. There was no sense in denying it to herself. As good as her I-don't-give-a-damn act was, she was mortified by what she'd said and done in front of Ian Douglas.

He laughed as he set down the stack of dirty dishes he had carried in from the dining room. "I think he didn't install a dishwasher because he and my mother had such fun doing the dishes together. They'd come in here after the evening meal and spend hours cleaning the kitchen. They'd talk and plan. I envied their closeness during those times."

Mollified by his refusal to take offense, Shay asked curiously, "Were you an only child?"

"Yes."

"Me, too. I think most only children feel left out

when their parents share a private moment. Excluded, like they're intruders and not really part of a family."

"Are you speaking from experience?"

She looked up at him from the sink, ready with a defiant answer, but his expression was soft with understanding. "Yes, I guess so," she admitted, then turned back to the sink while he made another trip to the dining room. When he returned, she asked the question uppermost in her mind without intending to ask it. All of a sudden it was there on her lips. "Why didn't you tell me you were a minister before I made a complete fool of myself?"

Again he laughed. "Circumstances weren't exactly conducive," he said, sweeping an old-fashioned straw broom around the vinyl floor. "When do you suggest I should have made such a pronouncement? While I was standing in the buff with my mouth hanging open? Or maybe you think I should wear a sign around my neck to warn people of my vocation."

He was making fun of her, and her every muscle strained in rebellion. "You could have said something about your work when we were talking this afternoon."

"What? And robbed you of the opportunity of trying to turn me on?"

Splashing hot water and suds against her stomach, she dropped a plate back into the sink and rounded on him. "I wasn't trying to turn you on!"

"Oh. So you run around without wearing any underwear just for the fun of it?"

"It's more comfortable than wearing ridiculously constricting garments designed by straight-laced Victorians." She pushed her anger aside and assumed a deliberately sultry expression. Leaning provocatively against the countertop, she looked up at him from under thickly fringed eyelids. "Minister or not, I see you noticed."

His blue eyes slashed down her body, leaving behind a trail of burning sensation. When they returned to meet her melting gaze, he shrugged indifferently. "I'd have to be blind not to." He took up a dustpan and knelt to sweep into it the debris his broom had collected. Furious, Shay turned back to the sink.

"You're a fine one to criticize what someone wears," she said. "I never saw a clergyman dressed the way you are." In casual slacks and an Oxford shirt, he looked like a tired executive from Manhattan who had come to Connecticut for a relaxing weekend. "You don't look like a minister."

Ian seemed highly amused as he raked the trash into the wastebasket. "How are ministers supposed to look?"

"Not like you," she insisted stubbornly. She could have said they should look older and softer. They should have kind, paternal features and white hair, and maybe steel-rimmed glasses. They definitely should *not* have coal-black hair that looked so satiny as to tempt a woman to run her fingers through it. They should not have blue eyes that pierced through the toughest self-defensive armors to read one's private thoughts. Those same eyes should not look at a woman with an intensity that seemed to burn her clothes away. Nor should a minister have a body that was tall and lean, hard and strong, tanned and dusted with dark hair.

Ian took up a dish towel and began to dry the dishes she had stacked in the drain. For several minutes they worked in silence. The house was quiet except for the soft clatter of dishes.

"What happened to our parents?" Shay asked.

When he wasn't being the stern judge, his smile was breathtaking. "They went for 'a turn around the property,' ostensibly to walk off their dinner. Personally I think it was to get away from us and indulge in some serious kissing."

"Why didn't they just go upstairs to their room?"

"That would be unseemly."

She laughed. "It's hard for me to imagine my mother behaving like a bride."

"Children rarely see their parents as sexual creatures."

"Do you mind?" She looked up at him, her head slightly tilted, aware of the curls rioting around her face.

There was a lengthy pause as he studied her. "Mind?" he finally asked hoarsely.

"About your father marrying my mother. You spoke very fondly of your own mother and the times the three of you spent here as a family."

He tossed the tea towel over his shoulder and carefully placed the stack of plates he'd dried in the cupboard in front of him. "Dad loved my mother very much. Celia told me the same thing about the relationship she had with your dad. Statistically it's the ones who were happily married who remarry quickly after the death of their mate. What your mother and my father have together now doesn't detract from their former relationships."

Shay considered the matter thoughtfully. "I like John, not only for the man he is, but also for the happiness he's brought to my mother. I never thought I'd see her this relaxed and content again."

"You don't resent him? You don't look upon him as someone trying to take your father's place?"

Shay smiled up at him, then turned away. "That's a very intuitive observation. As you might guess, I adored my father. At first I might have felt a twinge of resentment for the man who had replaced him in Mom's life, but not now. Not after meeting John and seeing them together. It would be selfish to begrudge her this happiness." She risked looking at him again. "What about you? Were you happily married?"

"Very."

"But you haven't remarried quickly."

His eyes met hers steadily. "No, I haven't."

Okay, so he didn't want to talk about it. They'd talk about something else. Feeling slightly rebuffed, she asked, "At what point in one's life does one decide to become a minister?"

"At what point does one decide to pose naked for a living?"

"Damn you!" she cried, whirling around and thumping him in the stomach with her fist. "I'm making every effort to be pleasant because this weekend is important to my mother and to John. I've tried to carry on a polite conversation, but at every opportunity you drop in some sly innuendo."

His hand whipped out to catch her wrist, and in one swift motion she was hauled against him. "Don't ever hit me again, and don't ever curse at me." His teeth were tightly clenched. "As for my sly innuendoes, I was asking out of a desire to know. What makes a pretty young woman want to sell herself the way you do?"

If he hadn't had her wrist clasped between fingers of iron, she might have been tempted to slap him. If she'd had the nerve. She was seeing full-scale the power of his temper. It was fearsomely intimidating and equally as restricting as his grip.

"Because I'm pretty all over, that's why," she said

loftily. "I was born with what some people consider a perfectly proportioned body. It has no blemishes, no scars, no birthmarks or moles. My body is far more striking than my face. That's why artists sometimes use my body even if they put another face on it."

She stopped to draw in a great breath and felt her breasts flattening against the solid wall of his chest. "It's a commodity, and that's what I'm selling. It has nothing to do with what's on the inside of me. You should revere the human body. It's God's creation. Some of the world's most fabulous artworks are nudes. The Vatican is full of them. Think about it, Reverend Douglas." She dragged her hand out of his grip, and fell back a step.

"What you say is true," he conceded, "but how can you live with yourself knowing that some . . . some pervert might make you the object of his sexual fantasies? Might look at your pictures and wish he could see you in the flesh, touch you, fondle you?"

"I can't be responsible for them! The people you're describing are rarely art enthusiasts. My pictures aren't sold on street corners by some vendor in a raincoat who accosts passersby with a 'Pst, pst, want to buy some filthy pictures?' As my mother hastened to explain, I don't pose for erotica." Instinctively, her better judgment clouded by anger, she arched her back and thrust her breasts toward him. "Besides, these aren't exactly the overgrown melons that would cause a hedonist to slaver, are they?"

The moment the words were out of her mouth, she realized what she'd done and resumed her normal posture. The softly swelling mounds of her breasts resettled on her chest. As she had said, they weren't very large, but were ripe with womanhood, delicately tipped, and beautifully shaped. Ian seemed to have a difficult time forcing his eyes away from them before he turned abruptly on his heels.

"All right," he said thickly, "you've made your point."

"Not quite." Fueled by rage, she seized the opportunity to put forth her opinion. Few people really understood her work. For some reason that was incomprehensible to Shay, it often made people question her morals. She usually looked upon such narrow-mindedness with a degree of amusement. But Ian's censure not only aroused her wrath, but also hurt her deeply, which made her all the more defensive.

Too, Ian Douglas's heart and mind might reside on a spiritual plane, but as evidenced by his barely suppressed fascination with her breasts, he had a carnal side just as everyone did.

"What do you think I do when I pose? Rush up several flights of dank, dingy stairs to a cold-water flat with poor lighting and peeling wallpaper? Do you think the *artist* and I engage in all sorts of prurient activities after I've posed in lascivious—"

"Enough, Shay!" he shouted, spinning to face her.

The hands he had sliced horizontally through the air froze at his sides. Her eyes locked with the blue ones over the tension-laden space between them. She didn't know which dumbfounded her the most, his overwhelming anger or his use of her first name. She stood shocked into mute immobility, holding her breath.

Had he been anyone else, she would have sworn he muttered a curse under his breath as he broke his frozen posture, turned away, and raked a hand through his hair. "No. That's not the concept I have of you or what you do," he protested. "It's unfair of you to label me as such a prude." He spun around to face her once again. "But what was I supposed to think? What kind of woman comes barging into a strange man's shower without the least bit of embarrassment?"

"Are you strange?" she quipped.

Her flippant retort only made him more angry. His hands formed hard fists at his sides. Deliberately she let her eyes travel down his body and up again. "The only thing I found strange about you was your choice of a song to sing in the shower. Knowing what you are, I'd have thought 'Rock of Ages' would be more appropriate than 'Good Vibrations.' "

She pulled the tea towel out of her waistband and

lifted a few stray strands of hair off her neck with a negligent hand. She wanted him to know that his anger was of supreme indifference to her.

"I happen to like the Beach Boys," he said. "Also the Beatles and the Bee Gees and Blondie. Now let me tell you what I dislike."

"I don't—"

"I don't like women who are so insecure about their femininity that they try to assume the masculine role. Granted, you've got a pretty body, but you were right when you said it had nothing to do with what's inside you. Because I don't think there *is* anything on the inside. I think you're just a beautiful shell surrounding a vacuum where the soul of a woman should be. You're so busy playing at being a somebody that you don't really know who or what you are."

She gasped in outrage. "Go to—" She broke off the last word when she remembered his warning. Then in defiance she yelled at him anyway. "Go to hell!"

She shoved the swinging kitchen door with unnecessary force. It banged against the dining-room wall as she stormed into the room. The noise caused John and Celia, who were standing just inside the front door locked in a passionate embrace, to jump apart, looking shamefaced and guilty.

"Oh, for pity's sake," Shay said in exasperation as she took the first few steps. "Why don't you two just go to bed and stop acting like morons?"

* * *

She thought that once she'd had a cool shower, brushed her hair and teeth, and climbed into the bed, she could dismiss what Ian had said as rubbish and fall into a dreamless sleep.

She'd been wrong downstairs, too, wrong to goad his temper, wrong to deliberately provoke his anger, wrong to curse at him. *Curse at a minister!* What was her problem? No wonder he thought so poorly of her.

Try as she did to block out his harsh words, they echoed in her head with the constancy of a waterfall. That they had been so close to correct made them all the more revolting.

Suddenly she heard the gentle closing of the bedroom door next to hers. Him again. Swearing that she wasn't interested in anything he did, she nevertheless listened avidly to the noises he made preparing for bed. When the house lapsed into stillness once more, she pounded the pillow, punishing it for her restlessness.

By what right did some rural preacher take it upon himself to point up all her personality flaws? Why should she care what he thought, what he said? Yet it wasn't so much his saying it, but the truth of what he'd said that anguished her.

She *did* play a role. For years she had felt empty inside, an emptiness that she couldn't put a name to but that seemed fathomless and impossible to fill. The body that had been preserved on canvas and in photographs was a valuable commodity, but it wasn't *her*. The husband she thought had loved her had actually been far more concerned about the way she looked and the things she did than with the way she felt and what she thought.

Anson Porter had been an ambitious young man on his way up the ladder of success in his accounting firm. His greatest goal was to achieve a full partnership in the company. He met Shay at an art exhibit. He wasn't there because he had an interest in art, but because one of the partners had sponsored a young painter who had done a series of nudes.

Shay, who was attending at the artist's invitation, liked Anson upon first being introduced to him. He asked endless questions about how the paintings featuring her had been conceived, how long she'd had to pose, etc. When he invited her for coffee afterward, she readily accepted.

That first date led to others, many others. They were happy; they were in love. When he proposed, Shay covered his face with ardent kisses. But soon after their whirlwind courtship and hasty marriage, it became apparent that even as Anson was grooming himself to become a full partner in the accounting firm, he was also grooming Shay to be his idea of what a full partner's wife should be.

She found herself driving a sedate car, dressing as

conservatively and unimaginatively as all the other wives, and attending luncheons and bridge tournaments that she found tedious and boring with women she found stupid and shallow.

"You're what!?" Anson shouted one night when she told him about a job she had gotten.

"I said I have a job posing for a sculptor. He's—"

"I don't give a damn who he is," Anson brutally interrupted. "You do mean pose naked, don't you?"

She gnawed her bottom lip and counted slowly to ten. "*Nude,* yes."

"Well, forget it," he said uncompromisingly. "What would everybody think?"

Vaulting out of her chair, she told him her opinion of what everyone would think. "You knew what I did for a living before we were married. It never bothered you then."

"*Before* we were married, not after. Un-huh, I'm not having my wife parade around naked in front of some dirty old man. I don't care how famous he is."

She exploded. "What a stupid, provincial, witless thing to say!"

"Maybe from your 'artistic' point of view, but not from the point of view of any self-respecting husband. Naturally I assumed you'd give up all this modeling stuff when we got married."

"Well, you assumed wrong, didn't you?" she said, stamping out of the room.

She didn't do that job. She gave in to Anson's arguments, but things were never the same between them. He had tried to stifle her lively spirit, the very thing that had attracted him to her in the first place. Or had he merely admired her body? Either way, he hadn't let her be what she was, but had tried to mold her into something she wasn't.

Everyone seemed to want to do that. Her mother wanted her to be a lady. Her husband had wanted her to be a society matron. What this Ian Douglas wanted of her she wasn't sure, but he didn't like her as she was.

What rankled most was that she wanted his approval, not approval of her body, which was easy to come by, but approval for the person she was. It was insane, it made no sense, yet she wanted him to like her. The thought persisted that for some reason she was attracted to him—not only to his body, though she'd never seen a man who appealed to her more. Something inside her seemed to cry out for something he had to give.

"You fool," she ridiculed herself in the darkness. "That's part of his job. He's supposed to inspire that kind of spiritual confidence." She dismissed the nebulous emotions he fired in her as no more than a response he'd cleverly manipulated, but even as she fell asleep, she wasn't convinced that's all there was to it.

* * *

The next morning she stood on the other side of the swinging kitchen door, listening to jovial chatter and the clinking of breakfast dishes.

For a moment Shay felt fierce resentment. Why had she bothered to come up here this weekend? The three of them were getting along famously without her. She had known nothing but torment all night, both in her dreams and during long periods of sleepless tossing. Ian Douglas was to blame.

A mischievous light began to dance in her dark eyes, and a smile tilted her lips. Damned if she'd let him make her odd man out and ruin her weekend. No doubt he'd pegged her as a rebellious hellion last night. What he was going to see today was a sweetly compliant stepsister whom he wouldn't recognize. Let him figure it out!

"Good morning, everyone," she called cheerfully as she breezed into the kitchen and kissed her mother's raised cheek.

"Good morning, dear. Did you sleep well?"

"Like a rock," Shay lied. She leaned over John and kissed him on the forehead. "Good morning, John."

"Shay, how lovely you look this morning."

"Thank you." Until now she hadn't glanced at Ian. Now she did. He looked far more virile, handsome, and sexy than any man of his profession had a right to look. Swallowing her timidity, she drew close to him, placed her hands boldly on his shoulders, and bent down. Her lips brushed his. "Good morning, brother."

The electricity that scorched her lips and sizzled through every vein had nothing to do with sisterly love. To the tips of her toes, she was aware of his masculinity, his scent, his feel, his size. All were testimonies to his manliness. Her body yearned for it, hungered for it, and she feared that he wasn't fooled for one moment by the childish game she was playing. She could even imagine that he felt the same current of arousal that she did the instant their lips touched.

But when she pulled back and stood erect, he stretched his long legs out in front of him and assumed a posture of utter indifference. "Morning, sis."

Shay's blood rose to a boil for an entirely different reason now, and her good intentions of a moment before flew out the window. "Why aren't you at prayers or something?" she demanded. "Isn't that what men of the cloth do?" Her sandals tapped smartly on the floor as she crossed to the stove. She heard her mother's sigh.

"I've already said my prayers," Ian responded levelly.

"I hope you said some for me." She flashed him a false smile as she splashed coffee into a cup.

"As a matter of fact, the many I said for you took up most of my meditation."

Shay tested the glass coffee pot's guarantee not to

break as she thumped it back onto the burner. "I didn't ask for—"

"John and I had the most wonderful idea," Celia interjected loudly, overriding Shay's scathing remark to Ian. "Why don't the four of us play tennis this morning before it gets too warm?"

"Tennis?" For a moment Shay's dislike for Ian was replaced by astonishment. She'd never known her mother to participate in anything requiring as much energy as tennis. "When did you learn to play tennis?"

"John's teaching me," Celia said shyly, looking lovingly at her husband. "Of course I'm not very good yet, but—"

"She's improving every day," he finished proudly. "What about it, kids? Are you up for a doubles match?"

"Did you bring your racket and tennis clothes, Shay?" Celia asked.

"Yes, though at the time I couldn't figure out why you suggested it."

"Wonderful," Celia said, clapping her hands happily.

"I don't know," Shay hedged.

"Maybe Shay feels self-conscious about her game," Ian suggested. "If she doesn't want to play doubles, you two—"

"I play a great game," she retorted angrily, interrupting his buttery drawl. Their eyes clashed. She knew hers were shooting sparks of irritation. His were guileless, but lurking just behind the innocent expression, she saw lights of amusement and victory. She'd fallen for the oldest ploy in existence.

"You men go change while Shay and I clear the table," Celia said, standing. "Shay, I know you don't usually eat breakfast, but those blueberry muffins are scrumptious."

"Thank you, Mom, but no. Coffee's enough."

"You're really far too thin."

"Now, Celia, leave the girl alone. It's chic to be slender," John said, surveying Shay's svelte form as Celia looked on.

"Then maybe you'd like my figure better if I lost a few pounds," Celia suggested, almost pouting.

John grabbed her and nuzzled her neck playfully. "I like your figure just the way it is."

Shay smiled at their display of affection, but she didn't want to admit how perturbed she was when Ian sauntered out of the kitchen. Though everyone else in the room had assayed her figure, he hadn't given it a glance.

John was right about her mother's figure. She looked cute as a button in her tennis togs. Her legs weren't as long, slender, or tanned as Shay's, but they were remarkably trim and firm for a woman her age.

The municipal tennis courts weren't as smooth as those found at country clubs, but they would suffice.

After they'd warmed up, the doubles match began. Tacitly, Shay and Ian became partners. He played well but methodically. His returns and serves were not spectacular. Celia was coached by a patient John, who didn't seem to care if they won as long as she was having a good time and not getting too tired. Shay relaxed, knowing she was playing better than anyone else. She didn't even push herself. It surprised her when Ian complimented her on a routine return and a less than fabulous lob.

"Good shot," he said laconically.

"Thanks," she returned in kind.

Except when necessary, they didn't look at each other. He certainly wasn't paying special attention to her, and she'd be damned before she'd stand before him like a tongue-tied teenager admiring his physique, which the tennis whites set off to full advantage.

What irked her was that she knew she looked good in her tennis outfit. It had a white halter top that left her back bare and showed off her tan. The white pleated skirt came to just below her hips. Beneath it her red trunks peeked out flirtatiously.

And this prude, this stick man, hasn't even noticed, she thought scornfully.

Before they had played a full match, Celia mopped

her brow with a handkerchief and said she'd had enough. "Why don't we go to the market and buy those steaks you wanted to grill while the children continue to play?"

"Great idea," John concurred.

Since Shay hadn't really exerted herself, she looked forward to having the whole court to herself. She nodded in agreement.

"We'll be back in half an hour," John called as he ushered Celia to the car.

"Want to rest a minute before we start?" Ian asked Shay as the car drove out of sight.

"I don't need to rest, but if you do, I'll be glad to wait."

"I'm ready," he said grimly, and without even tossing for it, chose the side of the court with the sun behind it. "You can serve first."

"Thanks so much," she said with dripping sarcasm, taking up several balls and moving to the service line. Warmed up from the earlier game with their parents, she zinged an impressive serve into his court. Before she knew what had happened, the ball was sailing in a straight line across the net to bounce within half an inch of the base line behind her. She muttered a curse.

"Was it in or out?" he called graciously from his side. Was he daring her to cheat and say it was out?

"In," she called back.

"I thought so."

Her mouth was set with firm determination when she applied all her strength to her next serve. It bounced with a spin in the corner of the box and ricocheted in the opposite direction. She didn't have time to gloat. The ball, parallel to the ground, shot like a fighter jet back across the net. She swung wildly, missing it by several feet.

Ian acted far too casual as he twirled his racket like a baton and whistled under his breath. So, she'd been suckered again. Was there such a thing as a tennis shark? Well, there was nothing to do but make the most of it, stay on her toes, and play as well as she could against an obviously superior player.

Though her serves were good, she scored only one point, and that one she felt Ian had given her. Not out of charity. The wicked arch of his brows told her he knew exactly what he was doing. He had given her the point only to heighten her mounting aggravation.

"My serve," he said after he'd won the game.

"I know the rules."

His grin was wide, disarming, charming; she wanted nothing more than to wipe it from his mouth.

"Bad loser?" he taunted.

"Just serve the damn ball."

He shrugged, overlooking her curse word. "Okay."

She never saw it. She saw his arm arc high over his head, saw him go up on his toes, saw his torso stretch, saw his arm sweep downward. The next thing she knew the ball was spinning away from her at a crazy angle.

"Fifteen love," he said in a deadpan voice. She would have much preferred him to shout with glee.

The next serve was just as hard, just as fast, just as lethal. "You're serving too hard," she shouted at him.

"You're not watching the ball. Keep your eye on the ball."

"The ball is a blur," she mumbled under her breath as she assumed her position.

"What did you say?" he called politely, postponing his serve.

"Nothing. Just serve."

The next shot flew dangerously close to her head. "Dammit, you're serving too hard! That thing could have killed me," she shouted.

"You're only mad because I'm aceing you. Do you want to quit?"

"No. But I'm not a target. Don't serve it so hard."

She could tell by his reach that the next one would be worse than the others. Furious, she dropped her racket and spun on her heels. "I'm not going to play anymore with a potential murderer."

Ian didn't have time to curb his momentum. He had overshot his mark, and the ball didn't even bounce before it slammed into the soft cushion of flesh that was Shay's behind.

She cried out sharply. Tears sprang to her eyes. The shocking pain made her nauseous. Her vision blurred. Pain, hunger, and too much sun all combined. She fell ignominiously onto the asphalt in a dead faint.

Chapter Three

I'm sorry, I'm so sorry. Shay, please forgive me. I didn't mean to hurt you."

The words were low and urgent, whispered and soothing. They fell on her ears like cool raindrops and coaxed her back to consciousness.

Not yet. She didn't want to open her eyes yet. For a self-indulgent moment she wanted to be coddled, held against the solid wall of this magnificent chest. She loved feeling his chin moving over her head. Her cheek and nose were being pressed into his damp, warm neck. He smelled of male perspiration mingling with a brisk cologne. That scent, the heat emanating from him, the hand that stroked her hair, and the lulling voice induced her not to awaken from her faint. It was far more pleasant to remain helpless and protected.

"I'm sorry, so sorry."

They were on the grass. She could feel it beneath her bare legs. Ian must have carried her off the court and cradled her in his arms as he sat down on the early summer grass, soft and green. How marvelous it was to be held securely in strong arms. Had she been given the choice, she might have chosen to stay there forever with his deep voice vibrating through her body with each heartfelt word and his hand—

She became aware of his hand. Not the one stroking her hair comfortingly. The other one. It was gently rubbing the area of her injury. Under her short skirt, with only the red tennis trunks between them, he was massaging her derrière. Gently he squeezed her, then his hand flattened, and he rubbed her with a slow, circular motion of his palm. And all the while he murmured his regret for having bruised and hurt her with his deadly serve.

She allowed her hand to wander up his ribs to clutch at the breast pocket of his knit shirt. The contoured muscles flexed and hardened beneath her hand. Then she lifted the screen of dark lashes from her eyes, and she was looking directly into his eyes. Their faces were inches apart as he bent over her.

He sighed his relief and closed his eyes for a brief instant before asking in a hushed voice, "Are you all right?"

She nodded, captivated by his nearness and the fragrant ghost of his breath which drifted across her face. "Yes."

"Shay, please forgive me. I'm sorry. I didn't mean to hurt you."

"I know." Why was she willing to absolve him so readily? She should be as mad as hell. Instead she was lying here, a victim of delicious lassitude, forgiving him with the benevolent generosity of a saint. To rail at him for his brutal game, which had finally resulted in her getting hurt, would require that she move away from him. Then he wouldn't be looking at her with unspeakable tenderness. His fingertips wouldn't be gliding over the features of her face as though he adored them. His other hand wouldn't be caressing—for there was no other word to describe the rhythmic stroking—the round fullness of her hip that even now throbbed with the impact of the rocketing tennis ball.

He couldn't forgive himself so easily. "I was well into the serve, watching the ball. I didn't see that you'd turned around until it was too late." He touched her cheek. "I'm sorry. I wouldn't have hurt you for anything in the world."

"But you were showing off," she said softly with a teasing smile.

"I was showing off," he admitted self-deprecatingly.

He grinned, and her heart expanded behind her breasts, causing them to swell and tingle. They were suddenly bursting with sensations she'd thought long dead. She'd buried those feelings after her marriage had ended in failure. Was that glorious breathlessness really there? Was it due to the accident or caused by something else much more significant?

He was gorgeous, if that adjective could be used on such a masculine face. Against the azure summer sky, which accented the color of his eyes, his hair shone raven black. Drawn into jagged furrows, his dark brows expressed his concern for her. A beautifully shaped nose, which was straight and slender only to flare slightly at the nostrils, formed a perfect bridge between his compelling eyes and sensuous lips. Shay wondered if the women in his congregation found it difficult to concentrate on the spirituality of his sermons as they watched that mobile mouth form the words.

The hip that wasn't being soothed by his hand rested in his lap. Beneath her bare thigh, she could feel his. It was hard and warm. The springy hairs that bristled from it tickled her skin. He had raised one knee to support her back. Her lightheadedness returned when she realized that her naked back was lying along his thigh.

Her eyes roamed avariciously over his face. She wanted to take as much advantage of the moment as she could. "You play tennis very well," she said, barely recognizing her own voice. It came through her lips like a seductive shadow.

He didn't answer for a long time. His eyes were

doing their fair share of greedy touring. He catalogued each of her features: brow, eyes, and nose came under his avid gaze. Then his eyes rested on her mouth and stayed. And stayed. They were still there when he said throatily, "Championship tennis team in college."

For long, portentous moments they didn't say anything, only looked, as though before now they had been starved for the sight of the other. The only movement was his hand, which still idly massaged the bruised spot. Almost imperceptibly his head moved closer. Her lips parted. His did the same. Her heart thudded in her chest—or was she feeling the pounding of his as she was pressed tighter against him?

Her hand crept up the collar of his shirt and slipped inside. "Ian?"

"Shay."

His face ducked lower. Even closer, closer. Her eyes focused on his mouth. She could almost taste its moist softness melding with hers.

She felt his body tense and go rigid at the same moment that he inhaled sharply. Reflexively the fingers on her bottom squeezed, then released her. His hand was yanked away as though it had been tugged upon by a malicious puppeteer. His head jerked upward, and she was dumped from his lap onto the grass as he jumped to his feet.

He stalked away from her to a nearby tree, where he leaned his forehead on the rough trunk. His whole body was trembling as his shoulders heaved with gasping breaths. Restless fists thumped against his thighs. His whole aspect was that of a man trying desperately to get a grip on control that was rapidly disintegrating.

Offended and hurt beyond measure, Shay stood up. She barely kept herself from falling when the injured hip almost failed to support her. The pain had diminished only to the level of a dull throb. Damn him!

"What's the matter, Reverend Douglas?" she taunted acerbically. "Did the scarlet woman almost tempt you to fall from grace? Heaven forbid that you kiss such a vile person as me."

He spun around, his physical agitation fueling his temper. His blue eyes were stormy. She could see it was an effort for him to speak in calm, level tones. "You'd better sit down and rest until our parents get back. You've just come out of a faint."

"And whose fault is that? You of all people should have heard about the meek inheriting the earth. You're nothing but a big bully. I'll have a horrible bruise for a month."

"No one would see it if you didn't—" He seemed about to say something, possibly something ribald, but he amended it. "If you didn't do what you do."

"How perceptive of you to realize that thanks to you I might not be able to work for several weeks."

"You have your job at the gallery."

"Which accounts for about half my income. I work strictly on commission and depend on my modeling jobs to carry me through the lean months."

"You could model *clothes*," he shouted. "But then that would be conventional, wouldn't it?"

"I don't look nearly as good in clothes as I do without them."

That thought seemed to make him nervous. His eyes scaled down her body, then looked quickly away. He wiped his palms on his white shorts. "You'd better sit down," he repeated in an unsteady voice. "You've had a shock."

"So have you, reverend. You've just discovered you're as human as the rest of us."

"I never professed to be otherwise."

"Oh, no, Saint Ian?"

"No," he said bitingly. "Why are you getting so riled, Shay? Because I didn't kiss you? Believe me, despite my work, I'm a man in every sense of the word. I'm a strong proponent of kissing. It's just that flamboyant, sexually liberated women don't appeal to me."

Rage washed over her, staining her whole body with a hot flush. "I didn't lure you down on the grass, you know. I woke up to find you fondling my fanny."

"I—" He faltered and swallowed hard. "I didn't realize what I was doing. You were hurt, and I was only . . . trying to determine how badly."

"Ha!" She laughed, tossing her head back. "You're a hypocrite, too. You were loving it."

Before he could make a rejoinder, they heard the crunch of tires on the gravel road and looked up to see John pull his car to a stop.

"All finished? Who won?" he called out the window.

"I did," Ian said unchivalrously as they made the short walk to the car.

"Shay, are you limping?" Celia asked as Shay opened the car door and climbed into the backseat. Ian didn't extend the courtesy of helping her.

She winced as she sat down. "Yes, I'm limping. Ian hit me with a tennis ball."

John, who was steering the car back onto the highway, slammed on the brakes, and both of the middle-aged people whipped their heads around to the backseat.

"Ian, you hit her with a tennis ball?" John demanded of his son.

"Accidentally," Ian said defensively. "She turned her back while I was serving. It was a dumb thing to do."

"Ian!" John barked.

"I was trying to save my life!" Shay shouted.

John looked from his son to Shay, and his gaze softened. "Are you all right? Where did the ball hit you?"

"Right in the butt."

Ian's words echoed in the close confines of the car, bouncing and rolling around the interior like balls on a roulette wheel before finally coming to rest. John stared at his son in mute surprise. Celia blinked rapidly in disbelief. Shay's head came around quickly to look at Ian with dismay. She didn't know which had surprised her the most, his forthright confession or his choice of words.

He turned to face her, and their eyes collided. To the further puzzlement of their parents, they both burst out laughing.

Their laughter may have dispelled the immediate animosity between them, but it did little to lessen the overriding tension. Ian treated her with deference. His excessive politeness irritated her as much as, if not more than, his previous condescension.

For the rest of the day he rarely allowed them to be in the same room together. When they were, if Shay caught him looking at her, he glanced away immediately. Considering the wide berth he gave her, she might well have been the Devil incarnate sent to compromise the soul of Ian Douglas. She felt like a character out of a Hawthorne novel.

After lunch Ian retired to his room to prepare for Sunday's sermon. "I have to leave early in the morning to get there in time for the church service," he explained.

Shay was surprised by how quickly the time had gone by. She had dreaded the weekend; now it was almost over. Of course she wasn't due to leave until Sunday evening, but spending the day in the cabin without Ian suddenly seemed a dismal prospect. It alarmed her that his departure would matter so much to her.

The afternoon afforded her the choice of either sitting alone in the house while Ian was sequestered in his room or accompanying her mother and John, who was going to try his luck fishing in a stream that cut through a corner of his property. Shay opted for the fishing trip.

The countryside was lush with the green of early summer. But with every step of the way to the stream, the twinge of pain in her hip reminded Shay of the tennis game that morning. As the afternoon ticked by, her anger increased.

For some reason she couldn't name she was incensed that Ian was determined to ignore her. From the moment she had seen him naked, water streaming down his body, he had been the foremost thought in her mind. She didn't want it to be that way, but it was. There was no use pretending otherwise. She was attracted to him as a man. Period. End of discussion.

That in itself might not be so noteworthy. But he

was the first man she'd been sexually attracted to since the breakup of her marriage. She'd gone on a few dates, usually arranged by friends who seemed bent on matching her with someone as soon as possible. Because of Shay's disinterest, these potential suitors had soon given up the chase and gone on to more promising pursuits.

"All right, Shay," she said to herself as she sat contemplating the rushing stream, "he's got a great body, and he's as handsome as a warrior angel. But he's diametrically opposite you as far as temperament and philosophy go."

Even the fact that Celia, with John's gentle encouragement, had successfully baited a fish hook couldn't distract Shay from her musings.

Forgetting Ian's physical appearance for a moment—if that were possible—she concentrated on the man he was. Why, when he represented the kind of person she had previously scorned, was she so attracted to him? Why had she thought she might very well die if he didn't kiss her that morning? Why did she still yearn to feel his lips against hers, to have his hands caressing her, not accidentally but with the full intent and purpose of loving her?

Then it struck her. Like a lightning bolt out of the blue, she realized that part of her attraction stemmed from the fact that he ignored her. Was that it? "Of course," she said aloud, then looked chagrined when Celia and John looked toward her curiously.

That had to be it. Shay Morrison was too intelligent, too worldly, too self-sufficient to believe that one look at a naked man, no matter how handsome, had left her as starry-eyed as a teenager. Love at first sight didn't happen. Besides, her feelings for the man were barely above detestation. Her curiosity was simply piqued because he seemed so *un*curious about her.

Yet she knew with every feminine instinct that he wasn't as impervious to her as he pretended to be. She chuckled as a plan for the evening began to unfold in her mind. They might never see each other again, but she'd be damned before she'd let Reverend Ian Douglas dismiss her completely from his thoughts.

"I think I'll head back, if you don't mind," she said, jumping up from her grassy seat on the bank. "I'm going to rest awhile before dinner."

"We'll follow shortly," her mother replied. "I'm bound and determined to catch a fish."

Judging from the high color in his face and his fidgety hands, John seemed to have other things in mind for when they were left alone in the woods. Shay was still smiling when she approached the house. She climbed the stairs and headed toward the partially opened door at the end of the hall.

She tapped softly on it. "Ian?"

There was a pause before he said, "Yes, come in."

She pushed the door open and arranged herself in its frame. The wide window on the landing was behind her. She knew golden sunlight was spilling around her like a halo, shining through her hair, bathing her skin with light. "I hope I'm not disturbing you," she said, hoping just the opposite.

"No. I've still go some studying to do, but I'm almost finished." He was sitting at a paper-strewn desk. A Bible and several research books lay open on it. A portable typewriter contained a piece of paper on which several lines had been typed.

"Mom and John will be along in a while." Why wouldn't he look directly at her? He seemed intent on mutilating a paperclip with fingers she could swear were nervous.

"How's the fishing?" he asked, glancing up. His blue eyes made a rapid inspection of her legs in the shorts she'd worn to the stream, and a lengthier inspection of her bare midriff below her halter top, before he dropped his eyes once again to the infernal paperclip.

"John had caught three when I left. Mom's still working on a bite."

"Good, good," he said in a voice that told her he didn't care any more about the results of the fishing expedition than she did.

"Do you need the bathroom?" she asked, stretching her arms lazily over her head.

"Uh . . . no," he said. "No."

"I'm going to take a nice long bubble bath before dinner." She dropped her arms and shook her body as though in eager anticipation of the sensual luxury of the bath. The motion caused her breasts to move bewitchingly beneath her top. A motion, if his dazed expression was any indication, that didn't go undetected.

"Fine. I don't . . . won't . . . you'll have the bathroom to yourself."

"Okay," she said offhandedly before she pivoted on her heel and left the doorjamb.

Minutes later, the tapping sound made by the keys of his manual typewriter came through the connecting door. That he was still able to work vexed Shay as she lay in the tubful of hot, bubbly water. But she smiled slyly when she recalled the uneasy look on his face each time his eyes had wandered in her direction. He was well aware of her as a woman. Even if his mind willed it not to be so, his body defied him.

Of course Shay didn't want to go any further than mild flirtation. She only wanted to pay him back for the times he had looked at her with tolerant amusement, much as one would look at a willful child. He deserved to be paid back for the humiliation he'd heaped on her.

When she was finished with her bath, making as many splashing noises as she could and humming "The Summer of '42" under her breath, she rinsed out her lingerie in the sink and draped each sheer, lacy article on the shower curtain rod. Though she usually slept in the raw, she'd brought along a nightgown in case her mother complained. It hung on a hook behind the door connecting to his room. Each time he reached for the doorknob, he would come in contact with the silky yellow fabric trimmed with ecru lace as fine as a spider's web. If he moved it, he'd have to handle it even more. Before leaving the steamy bathroom, she misted it heavily with her perfume.

She tapped on the bathroom door. The typing ceased abruptly. "Yes, Shay?"

"I'm all done now. The bathroom's yours if you need it."

"Thanks," was all he said, though it was a long time before she heard the typewriter again.

She knew her scheme had failed when he came down to dinner. John and Celia had returned in plenty of time to rest and clean up before the evening meal. As promised, John cooked succulent steaks and baked potatoes on an outdoor charcoal grill. Shay and Celia prepared a huge tossed green salad and all the trimmings.

Shay was ladling sour cream from the carton into a serving dish when Ian pushed through the swinging door smelling of soap and his distinctive cologne. "I'm starving. When's dinner?" The jauntiness of his walk and the carefree lilt in his voice worried her. He shouldn't be feeling nearly so cocky.

Celia laughed charmingly at him. "Just like your father. He's outside cooking the steaks. He said to join him when you came down. There's a beer for you in the refrigerator."

"Thank you."

As he crouched down in front of the refrigerator, Shay looked down at him over a bare shoulder. Her sundress had a straight bodice with nothing but strings crisscrossing at intervals for the back. The skirt was soft and full and fell to the middle of her calf. The ties of thonged sandals were wrapped around her ankles. The ethnic print of her dress accented the honeyed tone of her skin, made the blond streaks in her hair more prominent, and with the darker eye makeup she had applied, enhanced her exotic features.

"All finished with your studying?" she inquired in a sultry voice.

When his blue eyes lifted to hers, she immediately saw the mockery in them. With his powerful thighs he raised himself to his full height. She had to tilt her chin up awkwardly to look him full in the face. And what she saw she didn't like one bit. He was all but laughing at her!

"The panties you washed out weren't quite dry by the time I needed the shower, so I hung them on the back of a chair in your room. Hope you don't mind."

Then he strolled out the back door, letting the screen slam shut behind him. The crash punctuated his statement like a vaudevillian drumbeat.

"Panties?" Celia asked in a high voice. "Did he say—"

"Yes, panties, *panties*," Shay all but shouted at her mother. She turned back to her job, her whole body quaking with fury.

She was the victim of Ian's derision during the entire meal. He never said anything aloud, but his taunting glances told her he had caught on to her machinations, that he saw right through her designs, and that rather than thinking she was a seductress, he thought she was a highly amusing idiot.

She hardly touched the food on her plate, though she did full justice to the bottle of burgundy that John had opened to accompany their steaks. By the time she stood up to help her mother clear the dining-room table, her head was buzzing pleasantly. When they emerged from the cleaned kitchen, John and Ian were engrossed in a chess game. Celia settled down to watch a romantic movie on TV. Shay stewed.

Bored, she wandered listlessly from room to room. Spotting her tennis racket propped against the banister, she decided to take it back to her car. The cool evening air should help her muzzy head.

She planned to leave this bad experience behind her

early in the morning, even before Ian if possible, and return home. She would pack what she could tonight. Almost from the moment of her arrival she'd been made a fool of, and she couldn't wait to get back to her own world, where a few people even respected her opinion, thought she was pretty, and laughed with her instead of at her.

The car trunk lid popped up, and she was in the process of tossing the racket inside when she spotted her portfolio. She took it everywhere with her, like an appendage of her body. Inside the large, square leather folder was a history of her career as a nude model. She used the pictures of paintings, sculptures, and copies of photographs for reference when she interviewed with an artist for a job.

Now, almost crowing with glee, she hauled the heavy folder out of the trunk. Tucking the portfolio under her arm, she returned to the house.

She was alarmed to find her mother sobbing uncontrollably in John's arms. She dropped the portfolio onto the entry table. "Mom, what is it?"

"The movie," John said. Shay slumped with relief. "It ended sadly," he explained. "Come on, sweetheart, let's go upstairs." He kissed Celia on the temple and hugged her close as he negotiated the stairs for both of them. All the way to the top, he patted her back and repeated, "It was only a movie, darling."

Shay rolled her eyes heavenward, impatient with

her mother's sentimentality over a silly love story. Love. Didn't her mother know that love like that was manufactured by writers and composers? It didn't exist in the real world. But the sight of Celia and John, both obviously in love, leaning into each other for support as they reached the top of the stairs, contradicted her jaded outlook. The possibility that true love did exist was a disturbing thought.

Ian was standing next to her, also looking at her parents. When they disappeared, he glanced down at Shay. His expression was infinitely tender, as if he were looking at a newborn baby.

"Your mother epitomizes everything feminine," he said. Left unsaid, Shay knew, was that her daughter didn't. Ian returned to the couch and picked up the sports magazine he'd been reading. Slouching against the cushions and propping one jean-clad leg on the knee of the other, he seemed instantly absorbed by the printed page.

More than a little miffed because he was so rudely ignoring her, Shay stalked to the table in the foyer, picked up her portfolio, and plopped determinedly into the opposite corner of the sofa Ian was sitting on.

The leather cover thumped against the back of the couch as she opened the large book. The pages rattled as she arranged and rearranged the pictures, trying to attract his attention. Under her breath, but loud enough for him to hear, she commented periodically on each picture she held in her hand.

Finally he sighed heavily and turned toward her. "I guess I'm supposed to ask what you're looking at."

Why she didn't slam the book shut at that moment and go upstairs to her room, she didn't know. Possibly because something inside her chanted that sugar attracts more flies than vinegar. In any event, she smiled winningly. "This is my portfolio. Would you like to look through it?"

He shrugged, a gesture she found thoroughly annoying. Was he doing her a big favor by looking at pictures of her nude? Apparently he thought so. "Sure," he said in a voice that intimated he didn't have anything better to do.

Since he didn't move, she was forced to scoot along the couch, dragging the unwieldy book with her. He took it upon his lap and opened it, scanning the first series of pictures.

"I was still in college when these pictures were taken. That's when I first started posing. Dad had died, and money was tight. I was taking art classes, and one day the instructor asked me if I'd consider posing for the advanced art classes, which were already into nudes."

"A male instructor, I presume."

Her fingers itched to slap the knowing grin off his

mouth. "No, a female." Her voice was calm, hiding the anger that was nearly bursting from her.

She watched Ian's expressionless face as he slowly turned the pages of the book. His eyes moved over the pictures. He studied them with deep seriousness. But he could have been analyzing a brick wall for all the response he gave.

Wait until you get to the good stuff, she wanted to tell him. These first photographs were obviously unprofessional, taken by a friend so she could start her portfolio.

"This artist is famous," she said when he turned to a picture of a painting featuring only her back. Her hair had been swept up, leaving coy tendrils to trail down her neck. The smooth brush strokes had perfectly captured the texture of her skin. Shadowing had detailed the fragility of her spine and the impishness of the two dimples in the small of her back.

"Yes, I recognize his name," Ian said conversationally. "Didn't he do 'Morning Maid'?"

Shay looked at him in surprise. "Yes. I didn't think you'd know this artist."

"I don't know *him*, only his work."

He continued turning the pages, sometimes saying that he recognized a photographer or artist, commenting other times on the medium, never mentioning Shay, her pose, or her body.

"Which one is you?" he asked of a picture of a

sculpture that had been commissioned by the Fine Arts League of a major midwestern city to grace the fountain outside their new concert hall. It featured the Muses.

"The one with the lyre."

The toga covered only one breast. "Nice lyre," he said, nodding sagely. She could have cracked his skull.

Her heart began to pound when he looked at the painting of her on the beach. It was a nighttime seascape. The water was calm. A moon hung suspended in the sky like a china plate. The woman was posed in profile. She was leaning back, propped up by straight arms behind her. Her head was thrown back so that her back arched and her hair swept her naked back. Her knees were raised. She looked as though she were offering up her breasts to the moon, which was kissing them with iridescent light.

"This one is incredible. Absolutely beautiful," Ian said. She thrilled to the low, husky, reverent tone of his voice. He touched the picture. Her heart all but stopped when his fingers grazed over the breasts so beautifully painted. "Lovely," Ian whispered.

"Do you like it?" she asked tremulously, her throat tight with emotion.

"Yes, yes," he said earnestly. "I admire an artist who can reflect light off water that way and make it look so real."

She strangled on an outraged cry. He was admiring the painting, the technique. All the appreciation glowing in his eyes was for the artist, not the model. She stared at him, bewildered and wounded, but he didn't even notice. He was calmly turning the pages of the book.

"Here's another interesting study," he commented.

Shay dropped her eyes from his face to the black and white photograph. She lay stretched out on her back, knees raised. One languid arm had been lifted. The back of her other hand rested on her forehead. The photographer had backlit her so that the black outline of her body was in stark contrast to the bright light behind it.

The profile of her face and chin were clearly defined before they blended into the silhouette of her throat. The shape of her breast, the impudence of its nipple, was outlined in startling detail. Her stomach dipped into a graceful hollow. Beyond that, the softly swelling mound of her femininity blended into the top of her thighs.

It was a beautiful photograph of the female anatomy in silhouette. The anonymity of it made it all the more beautiful. It belonged to all women.

"This photographer often uses that backlighting effect, doesn't he?" Ian commented.

Who cared? She wanted him to notice the woman in the photograph, not the damn lighting. "Yes."

"I thought so. I've seen some of his other works. Did he do this one, too?"

The last photograph in the folder was the most recent, also the most suggestive. It had been shot for a perfume ad for the European market. It was far too bold for American magazines and billboards. It, too, was in black and white, but this time she was fully lighted. The camera was above her.

Her hair was spread out behind her head on black velvet. Her face was turned away from the camera, her chin almost resting on her shoulder. The photograph had been cropped to show only one breast covered with a sheer white veil. Through it, her nipple was enticing, yet oddly vulnerable.

But it was her expression that captured the attention of the viewer. It was sublime. Her eyes were closed, her brows slightly puckered, her moist, shiny lips parted in a hint of a smile. Its message was clear: this woman was in the throes of passion fulfilled.

Actually at the time the photographer had said, "When we finish, Shay, I'll treat you to a hot fudge sundae. Think of it. Gooey chocolate, whipped cream, almonds, vanilla ice cream."

His camera had been clicking all the time he talked. She closed her eyes and licked her lips in anticipation since she hadn't eaten that day. When she heard his whispered, "My God," she knew she'd given him just the expression he'd been striving for all afternoon.

Ian studied the photograph for a long time. Shay's heart stood still. She had a wild vision of him slinging the picture, the book, and his conscience aside, grabbing her to him, and devouring her mouth with his. She saw her fingers plowing through his thick black hair to hold him fast, saw herself reclining at his insistence on the soft cushions of the couch, saw him stretching out above her, saw his hands urgently but gently peeling away her clothes. Blood pounded through her veins as her fantasy enlarged and she saw his hands exploring her, saw him raining hot kisses on her naked skin. She wet her lips.

Ian stirred, and she held her breath. Hold me, kiss me, she wanted to cry out to him.

Instead he carefully stacked all the photographs neatly and closed the cover of the portfolio. "They're all very good. I'm sure you have a long career ahead of you—provided you don't get fat or anything."

She wanted to scream, to weep. But she only sat there stupefied as he pushed himself to his feet, stretched, and yawned broadly. "Boy, I'm tired. If you'll excuse me, I'm going to bed. Don't forget to turn out all the lights before you come up. Good night."

Chapter Four

S he sat in the empty room, feeling more alone than she had ever felt in her life. Was it too much to ask that they indulge in a little harmless kissing? Would that have offended his stern principles so very badly?

Irritated now, she picked up the portfolio and dumped it onto the table near the front door so she wouldn't forget it in the morning. "Thanks for nothing," she muttered.

Lacking anything better to do, and not yet ready to go upstairs, she wandered into the kitchen for a glass of milk. She spied the bottle of burgundy on the counter. It was much more appetizing than a glass of milk. Pouring a liberal portion into a glass, she downed it in a few stinging gulps.

"Damn him, damn him, damn him." If she couldn't curse him in his presence, she'd do it while alone. It's not as if I'm a tramp or anything, she thought to herself. She wasn't promiscuous, as he seemed to think.

If only he knew how monastic her life really was. She hadn't had any kind of relationship with a man since her divorce.

Wiping angry tears from her eyes, she poured herself another glass of wine. "All I wanted of you, Ian, was a little affection," she said between swallows that drained the glass. A few harmless kisses and caresses. Would that have offended his rigid moral code? Was he totally turned off by sex? Or was he just totally turned off by *her*? A sound resembling both a hiccup and a sob escaped her lips as she poured the last of the wine into her glass. Didn't he find her the least bit attractive, the least bit desirable?

She didn't consider why she wanted Ian when other men had tried to gain her affection and failed. In the far recesses of her mind she knew that finding the answer to that question might prove to be dangerous. She couldn't handle such introspection now.

Having drunk more tonight than she ever had in her life, she swayed as she turned toward the dining-room door. It wasn't hanging straight. She'd have to tell John about that in the morning. He really should do something about that uneven floor, too, she thought disjointedly as she groped her way to the stairs, instinctively obeying as she went Ian's instructions that she turn out the lights.

How long it took her to climb the stairs, she never could remember. The next thing she knew, she stood staring blankly at the door of her room. Something, a mischievous brain wave that hadn't been dulled by the wine, caused her to look farther down the hall to the other door, a twin to hers, that led into Ian's bedroom.

Chuckling softly, she tipsily negotiated the few steps that brought her to the door. She opened it quietly. The room was dark, but moonlight filtering through the window allowed her to see his sleeping form beneath the light blanket on the double bed.

An idea so inspired that she had to cover her mouth to keep from laughing out loud burst like a ray of light on her fogged mind. It would serve him right, she thought vindictively. It would rattle him, shake his damn cool attitude, blow his pious condescension to hell.

Trying to stabilize the spinning room, she weaved toward the bed. Her dress was no problem. It slipped off easily. As did her underwear. The straps of her sandals were a challenge to her rubbery fingers, but soon they had joined the pile of clothing on the floor. Giggling like a child about to commit the naughtiest of no-nos, she raised the covers and slid naked between the sheets.

His body was warm. That was her first thought as she laid her head on the pillow beside his. He was facing away from her, but she could hear his steady breathing. Resting her chin on his shoulder, she lifted a hand, intending to put it around him. She longed to touch the mat of dark hair that covered his chest, to comb her fingers through it, to satisfy her curiosity about its texture.

But her arm seemed to weigh a ton, and her hand remained heavily on his hip. A warm, sweet lethargy seeped through her body like melting butter. The roaring in her head had quieted to a lullaby. Sleepily she wondered what his congregation would think if they knew their sanctimonious pastor slept naked.

Then an alcohol-induced sleep stole every conscious thought.

Was this a dream or was it really happening? Shay didn't open her eyes on the outside chance that it was nothing more than a wonderful dream. It certainly felt real, but the probability of it was so outlandish she feared it was only a product of her imagination.

She was lying entwined with Ian in a bed. One of his arms was beneath her neck. Her head rested in the crook of his elbow. The other arm was holding her firmly against him. His hand idly traced her spine. She could feel the pressure of his leg on top of hers, moving languorously, detailing the contrasts between them. One of her legs was positioned between his thighs, her knee tucked snugly against their juncture.

Ardent lips planted a kiss at her hairline and trailed down the side of her face. He kissed her temple at its tenderest spot. He blessed her high cheekbone with soft kisses. Her ear knew the sweet nuzzling of his mouth, the explorations of his tongue. Then her neck was treated to small, quick kisses by parted lips. The stubble on his chin abraded her pleasantly.

Acting on instinct, she lifted her arm around his neck. She didn't need to open her eyes. By feel she laid her arm on his shoulder, and her fingers were finally granted the privilege of threading through his glossy black hair.

Her raised arm provided him access to the front of her body. He seized the advantage. His hand slid around her and glided up her narrow ribs to lightly cup her breast. He sighed, his breath a moist vapor on her neck.

He fondled her tenderly, adoringly. Questing fingers lightly brushed her nipple, plucking it gently until it bloomed with desire.

A satisfied male growl rumbled in his throat as his mouth worked its way up to hers. Their lips met. For a long moment they were still. Their lips were closed as they pressed together. That was enough. But not for long.

At the same instant, ravenous hunger overcame them. Their mouths opened greedily, seeking to appease and to be appeased at one and the same time. His tongue plunged deeply into the soft recess of her mouth to thoroughly explore and investigate. It toyed with the tip of hers. When it tired of playing, it thrust again boldly into the wet, silky harbor of her mouth.

His hand on her breast became more possessive and much more arrogant in its caress. He fondled the smooth plumpness and rubbed his fingers against the delicate peak. Her nipple firmed to a hard bud of awakened passion between his gently squeezing fingers.

Shay purred her contentment, drew her arm more tightly around his neck, and pressed her knee higher, which acquainted them both to the strength of his desire. She moaned with longing and arched closer to the rigid flesh.

His eyes sprang open, and he froze.

He stared at her in horror and incredulity as she sleepily opened her eyes and smiled at him. For an endless span of time, while the seconds ticked by ponderously, he only stared at her, wide-eyed and still.

Then in one swift motion he pushed away from her and rolled off the bed. The sheet became entangled in his legs, and he kicked at it furiously. It came off her body, leaving her lying there completely exposed to his glazed eyes. She was disoriented by his sudden motion and couldn't yet understand what had happened.

"What—?" He looked around him wildly as though trying to establish where he was.

Shay loved the sight of his magnificent body and

the mussed unruliness of his black hair, but she wished he wouldn't shout. She had a pounding headache and a burning, sour sensation in the pit of her stomach. Groggily she sat up, raising a hand to her head in an effort to stop the blinding pain.

"What are you doing here?" he demanded in a shout that might just as well have been crashing cymbals in her head.

With bleary eyes that refused to focus clearly, she looked up at him. "Sleeping. Until you started kissing me." She held out a beseeching hand. "And please don't shout."

"I wasn't shouting. Do you think I want to wake everyone up? And I wasn't kissing you."

"Oh, yes, you were," she insisted, smiling up at him. At least she thought she was smiling. She seemed to have little control over her muscles. Lord, her head hurt. And why was it so bright in there? "Would you please draw the curtains clo—"

"I wasn't kissing you," he repeated, pushing each word through his teeth. "That is, I didn't know I was. I was dreaming and you . . . you . . ." His words faded to an agonized moan as he turned away and covered his face with his hands. That his eyes hadn't been able to stay off her reclining form was reason enough for the conflict inside him. "I can't believe this."

She closed her eyes against each blasting word that seemed to splinter into her ears straight to her brain.

She wanted to scream at him, but all her vocal cords could manage was a hoarse croak. "Nothing happened. You're getting angry all over again for no reason."

When he spun back around, he was almost snarling. "Angry! I could easily murder you." He ripped the sheet off the bed and wrapped it around his waist, knotting it clumsily.

She bolted off the bed, heedless of her own nakedness and sparked to life by his indignation. "Why?"

"Why?! *Why?*" He was shouting now. "You compromised everything I stand for, that's why. Only an easy tramp climbs in bed with a man, especially with a man who's given her no encouragement."

Without thinking, she swung her arm wide, and her palm cracked against his cheek. At that moment the door opened behind them. "Is something wro—?" Celia's concerned question died on her lips. Her eyes bounced from her naked daughter crouched over the bed as if she were about to be sick to the enraged minister who was also naked save for a sheet wrapped around him and Shay's red handprint on his cheek. Celia gave a choked gasp and pressed trembling fingers to her chalky lips.

Ian lunged toward Shay, grabbed the blanket from the bed, and wrapped it around her. But his strong arms were too great a temptation to her weakened body and whirling mind: Despite the insulting, inaccurate name he had called her, she slumped against him, clutching at the sheet around his waist to maintain her balance.

At that moment, John arrived in the doorway, pulling his robe on over his pajamas. He stared at the scene before him in mute astonishment.

"Dad—" Ian began.

"Son, how could you?"

"Please don't shout," Shay mumbled miserably.

"I didn't do anything," Ian retorted. "She did." He thrust Shay away from him and, when she swayed drunkenly, forced her down on the side of the bed. The impact sent a jolt of pain up her spine to explode out the top of her head. She groaned in agony. "She was in bed with me this morning when I woke up."

Celia hiccuped a sob and buried her face in her hands. "Celia, I swear to you," Ian said earnestly, "that I didn't do anything improper with your daughter."

His placating words pierced through Shay's dazed mind, and she snapped her head erect. "Well, it wasn't because you didn't want to, pastor." She lurched to her feet. "Whether you admit it or not, you were kissing me." She stopped to swallow and shuddered with nausea.

The room was spinning around her. Ian's blue eyes were hard with accusation as he glared down at her. "Your hands were all over me. You kissed—" She tried again to tell him in no uncertain terms just what she thought of him, but nausea rose in a sickening wave. It seemed to take forever for her to reach the bathroom and slam the door behind her.

Pale and weak, she made her way downstairs. Her knees threatened to buckle at any moment. Though arrows of pain were still shooting between her temples, her head felt light and woozy. She had no idea what to expect when she arrived in the kitchen. The uproar in Ian's room had gone on for several minutes after she'd fled for the bathroom. When it had finally quieted, her mother had knocked on the door.

"Do you need any help, Shay?" she'd asked.

"No."

Celia had taken her at her word. After washing her face in cool water, brushing her teeth, and pulling her hair back with a barrette, Shay had gone to her room to dress. She had heard the other room being vacated as one by one everyone went downstairs.

In the light of day, with her brain not influenced by alcohol, she admitted that her behavior had been utterly childish and inappropriate, and she didn't blame Ian in the least for being furious. He was a minister, after all, and though nothing had happened—not much anyway—he had to live above reproach. His reputation mustn't be tainted in the slightest degree. It was obvious from everything he said and did, by the way he conducted himself, that he was dedicated to his work. What right had she to tamper with his life?

In addition, she suspected that his pride had suffered as much as his conscience. He had been a victim of circumstance, therefore not wholly accountable. But he was also a man who, she guessed, would want to be in charge of any situation, especially those involving women. She'd deprived him of that advantage, and that as much as anything had probably fired his temper.

It was the hardest thing she'd ever had to do to push open the door to the kitchen. But she swallowed her last ounce of pride and went through. The hushed conversation ceased abruptly. The atmosphere was thick with tension. More than anything, she regretted having ruined this weekend for her mother and stepfather.

In the heavy silence she crossed to the coffee pot on the stove. Her hand wasn't quite steady, but she managed to half-fill a mug. She took a tentative sip. After one more she turned to face them.

"I'm sorry. I created a ruckus, and I'm sorry." John wouldn't quite meet her eyes when she addressed him. "I want to apologize for ruining an otherwise delightful weekend." They never need know she'd had a miserable time. "Mom, I'm sorry to have embarrassed you in front of your new family." Looking at a point somewhere off Ian's right shoulder, she said, "It's not her fault that I behaved so badly. All my life she's been trying to make me a lady of some discretion. It's not her failure, but my own."

"Shay, dear." Her mother jumped to her feet and embraced her. "I love you just the way you are. Don't ever feel you have to apologize for who you are. It's just that sometimes you act rashly and irresponsibly."

"Yes, I do."

She patted her mother's hand and urged her to sit back down at the table. "Reverend Douglas, Ian, I had too much wine after you went up to bed. What seemed like a fantastic practical joke last night . . ."

Her voice trailed off lamely, and for the first time she looked fully at him. She was shocked to see neither censure on his face nor anger. Nothing really, except a faint light glowing in his blue eyes. What it meant she didn't know.

"I overreacted and behaved badly," he said tersely. "What happened last night was your fault. What happened this morning was mine," he added in a softer tone. "I kissed you while I was dreaming. I'm sorry to have taken advantage."

Scalding tears welled up in her eyes as she stared at him in wonder. He was taking the blame for their lovemaking—and there was nothing else to call it— on himself. Why, when he'd ridiculed her all weekend, was he now forgiving her so generously? Her eyes probed the depths of his. Could she detect understanding there, or was it simply that she wanted so badly to see it?

He pushed back his chair. "I need to go if I'm to get to church before the first hymn," he said, grinning at John and Celia, who seemed vastly relieved that whatever had transpired between their children had been resolved.

Shay noted then that he was dressed in a dark gray three-piece suit with a white shirt and a tastefully dotted tie. His suitcase was standing just inside the back door.

"Dad, it was great. Sorry I won't be here to eat the fish you and Celia caught yesterday."

"Next time," John said, hugging his son unselfconsciously and thumping him proudly on the back.

"Celia," Ian said, taking Shay's mother in his arms for a fierce hug. "You're good for the old man," he said, teasing. "Don't let him take you for granted." He kissed her noisily on the cheek.

"Shay." Just the sound of her name coming from his mouth stopped her heart momentarily, then sent it jumping to her throat. "It was a pleasure to meet you." He extended his hand, and mechanically she reached for it and pumped it twice before letting it go.

He turned away and went to the door, leaning down to pick up his suitcase. She had an overwhelming compulsion to run to him and throw herself into his arms. But, of course, she didn't. The weekend was over. They'd rarely see each other again, if at all.

"Drive carefully," Ian's father called to him as they waved good-bye.

Once he was out of sight, Celia and John turned back into the kitchen. Celia's smile collapsed when she saw Shay leaning against the countertop. "Shay, are you still ill?"

Shay shook her head absently and forced her feet to move. They seemed cemented to the floor. "No, just a little shaky. I think I'll go upstairs and lie down for a while. Then I need to be on my way."

She left about noon, after her mother had forced her to eat a scrambled egg and a slice of dry toast, and drink two cups of tea sweetened with honey.

During the drive home, Shay tried to diagnose her ailment, but couldn't. It was more than a hangover. Suddenly she didn't care about anything. Living seemed to be too much trouble to bother with. It required too much energy. Often it inflicted pain. The possibility that Ian Douglas had something to do with her malady flickered on the outskirts of her mind, but she refused to contemplate that thought further.

She returned to work, having convinced herself that the weekend rest in the country had done her a world of good. She didn't have any modeling jobs lined up, so with a burst of enthusiasm, she threw herself into her work at the gallery.

Hans Vandiveer, a wisp of a man with prissy manners and a pointed goatee, was pleased. "Watch out or I may turn all the difficult-to-please customers over to you," he warned her, wagging a slender finger in her face.

She'd worked in his shop for three years, but knew little about him except that he lived alone with four cats, whom he talked about as other people did their children. If he'd ever had a meaningful attachment in his life, male or female, he'd never mentioned it. Shay thought it safer not to inquire and was glad she didn't know. He was pleasant enough to work for as long as she could overlook his fanaticism about keeping his shop and storeroom neat.

His demand for cleanliness was the reason why Shay was perched atop a ladder, dusting a shelf that displayed inexpensive reproductions of Stuben and Lalique glass sculptures. It was mid-August, six weeks since the brief time she'd spent in the country. Shop windows displayed back-to-school clothes and supplies. Though the weather was still mild, several recent chilly mornings had warned of the approaching fall.

Shay had talked to her mother at least once a week since that weekend in late June. Celia had telephoned that following week to report that she and John were back in Trenton.

"We spent a few extra days at the cabin."

"I don't blame you. It was lovely."

"We heard from Ian. He made it in time for church, but the compressor on the church air conditioner had gone out. He said it was too bad he hadn't prepared a sermon on hell for that morning."

Shay had laughed as she knew she was expected to, though she'd wondered why the mere mention of his name could set off such conflicting emotions in her as resentment and joy.

Now she gave the glass elephant one last swirl of the feather duster. She was lowering her foot to the next rung of the ladder when she heard the tinkling sound of the bell, which signaled that a customer was entering the shop. Over her shoulder she called out, "I'll be right with you."

"No rush."

At the sound of his voice her heart pounded and her hands gripped the sides of the ladder. Her careful footsteps down the rungs faltered. She took a deep breath and looked toward the door.

He was standing a few steps inside, dressed in a pair of gray slacks and black loafers. The collar of his cream-colored sport shirt was open beneath a navy blazer. His hair was boyishly windblown. Inexplicably she felt like crying.

His eyes caught hers in an inescapable, invisible net and held them as she remained perched motionless on the ladder. "Hello, Shay," he said at last.

"What are you doing here?" Wasn't that what he'd asked her when he'd leapt out of bed that morning?

He shrugged, and one corner of his mouth lifted into a smile of chagrin. "I thought I'd offer to buy you a cup of coffee."

Chapter Five

A traitorous jubilation filled her heart and set it to dancing. She had every reason in the world to dislike him for all the fun he'd poked at her. He was a self-righteous, judgmental prude. For the life of her, she couldn't understand why her mouth had gone dry, why her hands and knees were suddenly shaking, why she found it impossible to take her eyes off him, and why, rather than casting off the happiness that bubbled inside her, she relished it.

Don't be a fool again, Shay, she cautioned herself, lassoing her soaring heart. Flashing him a stepsisterly smile, she took the last steps down the ladder and set her featherduster aside. "You came all the way from . . ."

"Brookside."

"Yes, Brookside. To buy me a cup of coffee?"

He smiled again, wider this time, more disarmingly. "I was thirsty. What time do you get off?"

"Vandiveer left early today. I'm closing the shop."
She consulted a brass clock on the wall. "In about a
half-hour."

"Do you mind if I wait?"

Still dazed by his unexpected appearance, she
shook her head. She couldn't believe he'd really driven
all that way for a coffeebreak, just to see her.
Maybe . . . Oh, no. "Ian, there's nothing wrong, is
there? My mother? John?" She had taken several anxious steps forward to clutch at his coat sleeve, convinced that he'd come to bring her news of disaster
and was trying to ease into it, to cushion the blow.

His large hand covered hers where it lay on his
forearm. "No! I promise. They were fine the last time
I spoke with them a few days ago. I meant it when I
said I came to see you."

"Oh . . . good," she said automatically. Her mind
wasn't on what she was saying. She was thinking how
wonderful it was to look at his face. His eyes were ex-
ceptional. She'd never seen eyes that were such a startling blue. Raven black and unruly, his hair curled
crisply about his head. When silver began to show up
in it, he'd be even more handsome. His mouth was
masculine but had a sensitivity that was rare in so virile a face. She knew his mouth was capable of tenderness. When he'd kissed her . . .

Don't think about it, don't think about it.

They'd been staring at each other for a long while,

and her hand was still trapped beneath his. Taking a step backward, she lowered her eyes nervously and pulled her hand away. Any resultant awkwardness was spared them when a customer entered the shop.

As Shay helped the woman with her selection of a porcelain ashtray, Ian amused himself by gazing at the artwork on the wall. Out of the corner of her eye, while pretending to be interested in the woman's chatter about the color scheme in her living room, Shay watched him.

His posture was proud and straight. He commanded respect by virtue of his evident physical strength. Weren't ministers supposed to engender spirituality rather than carnality? Ashamed as she was to admit it, every time she looked at him, her thoughts ran closer to the latter.

"Thank you and come back," she said as the cash register's ding signaled the conclusion of the sale. The lady carried out her purchase, and they were left alone again.

"You look different here than you did at the cabin," Ian stated, making a long, thorough appraisal of her.

She was dressed in a caramel-colored skirt that was full and soft. Her blouse was of a harmonizing color in georgette. A chaste bow was tied at her throat. Pale stockings and low-heeled shoes completed the prim and proper ensemble.

"Well, I should hope so," she said, laughing to

screen the breathlessness his visual tour of her had brought on. Instead the sound came out in short, staccato puffs. "Mr. Vandiveer is very strict about the image we project. Most of our customers have conservative tastes."

"I like you this way."

"You do?"

"But I liked you the other way too."

"You did?"

"Yes." He stared down at her for an unsettling moment before he added with low, urgent sincerity, "Very much."

She could only look at him in dumbfounded confusion. Her responses had sounded like a wind-up doll's. "You do? You did?" Lord! She was behaving like an idiot, and she couldn't stop it. Her brain had turned to mush. Beneath her clothes, her body was hot. The room seemed to close in around them, to squeeze them together. It was so unbearably quiet. All she could hear was the unsynchronized ticking of the numerous clocks they had on display.

The air became thick with . . . with *something* going on between them. She couldn't pinpoint it. She'd never experienced it before with a man. Nothing had prepared her for it. Her breath came in rapid pants and seemed inadequate to fill her lungs.

She was saved from embarrassing herself by the arrival of another customer, who came rushing in, explaining hurriedly that he'd just got off the train from Manhattan and realized that this was his wife's birthday and that he didn't have a present.

"I'm sure we'll find something she'll like," Shay said calmly. She risked a glance at Ian, who was smiling at her as though they were sharing a secret.

By the time she'd helped the man with his selection and gift-wrapped it for him, her nerves were frazzled. She followed the customer to the door and turned the needlepoint CLOSED sign to the outside. "That's the last customer I want to deal with today," she said, leaning wearily against the door. "Is your offer for that cup of coffee still good?"

"You bet."

She secured the shop for the night and gathered her purse and jacket. When they stood facing each other on the sidewalk, he asked, "Where to?"

"Oh, let's see." She hadn't given any thought to where they could go. There weren't many restaurants in town, and she couldn't think of any place suitable. "Well . . ."

"Do you have a coffee pot?"

Startled, she looked up at him. "You mean at home?" He nodded, and her heart tripped over itself on its rolling journey to the bottom of her stomach. "Yes. Would you just as soon go to my apartment?"

"That sounds like the best solution. Unless you'd rather not."

"No, no that's fine. It's just . . ."

"What?" he probed.

She shook her head. "Nothing." He'd taken her totally by surprise. Should a man in his position invite himself to a single woman's apartment? "I walk from here. Is that okay?"

"Fine."

The light was still strong, although shadows were lengthening. Shops along the sidewalk were closing for the night. Commuters were rushing home. Walking beside Ian, Shay was seeing things she'd never noticed before, hearing sounds, paying attention to smells. It was as though all her senses had suddenly awakened after a long sleep. She breathed deeply, knowing a full and satisfied feeling inside her that she hadn't known for years. Was it contentment, joy, peace? She wasn't sure, and its name didn't matter. She only wanted to take delight in it while it remained.

To fill the silence between them as they strolled toward her apartment, she said, "Mom told me about the broken air conditioner in your church. Did you get it fixed?"

"With my own bare hands and a few choice words." He laughed.

"You're kidding!"

"About what? Fixing the air conditioner or the few choice words?"

"Both."

He regaled her with anecdotes about his constant hassles with the querulous air conditioner, and by the time they reached her apartment they were laughing easily.

"Here we are."

The stately old house was set like a matriarch on a tree-shaded lot in the middle of a street lined with similar houses. It had three stories, if you didn't count the basement. Tall windows flanked a front door decorated with a heavy brass knocker. The wide front porch was lined with thick shrubbery. The roof was dramatically pitched and gabled.

"All this belongs to you?" Ian asked in surprise.

Shay laughed. "Just the corner apartment on the second floor. Come on."

She led him up the steps to the porch and through the front door. Their footsteps were muted by an ancient Persian runner as they climbed the majestic staircase to the second floor.

At the landing Shay turned toward the door with a discreet 2 stenciled on it. After unlocking it, she went inside ahead of him. She gave a hasty glance around and breathed a sigh of relief. She'd left things in some order that morning.

"This is great," Ian said with admiration as he looked around him. The room was positioned in the corner of the old house, and its two bay windows overlooked the front lawn and were filled with plants. There were no curtains or drapes. The living area was spacious. Shay's knack with color was reflected in the tastefully chosen sofa and easy chair, the framed prints on the walls, the rug covering only a center square of the oak floor, and the variety and combinations of textures. "I like it," Ian said. "Does the fireplace work?"

"When I can afford the wood," she replied. "The bedroom's through there." She pointed toward a partially closed door. "It has a wide window, too. And the kitchen is through here. I'll get the coffee started."

Nervously she scurried toward the tiny kitchen, dropping her purse and jacket on a chair. It had suddenly occurred to her that Ian Douglas was the first man ever to stand inside the door of her apartment. Many had begged for the privilege. All had been refused admittance.

"How long have you lived here?" Ian called.

"Since—" She bit off her sentence, then realized that that kind of reticence was silly. "Since my divorce. About three years."

He followed her into the kitchen. Glancing over her shoulder, she noticed that he'd taken off his coat. Her fingers fumbled as she spooned coffee grounds into the filtered cup of the coffeemaker.

"Why didn't you choose to live in New York? Isn't that where you lived when you were married?" He took a seat at the round table, which was only large enough for two chairs.

His ease at making himself at home discomfited her. She was sure this was only a friendly call, perhaps to smooth the troubled waters between them for their parents' sake. He looked upon her as a stepsister whom he'd have to learn to tolerate.

But she didn't see him that way. His presence was crowding her heart and mind just as his large body was crowding her tiny kitchen. Up until then her small domain had remained inviolate, as had her heart. Now neither would ever be the same.

Squelching her nervousness, she replied to his question, "I like New York City. I enjoy going periodically. It's exciting, energizing. But I'm always glad to come back home." She took cups and saucers from the cabinet, trying hard not to look at the long legs stretched out over the linoleum floor. She tried even harder not to remember how they looked in tennis shorts. "Besides, if I lived in the city, an apartment like this, even if I could find one, would be exorbitantly expensive. And I prefer trees and grass to concrete. Do you use cream or sugar?"

"Black."

The coffeemaker seemed determined not to drip. She glared at it, willing it to work so she wouldn't have to stand there not knowing what to do with her hands.

"You don't have any paintings or photographs of yourself on the walls."

Turning in the narrow space to face him, she brushed her skirt against his pants leg. "No, I don't." Was he going to start mocking her again, taunting her, rebuking her for her modeling? "There's one painting in the bedroom. I gave it to Anson for a wedding present. When we split up, I asked for it back."

"Yes. I can see why you'd want to do that." He avoided her eyes, and she turned back to the coffeemaker.

"It's ready," she said, hoping her relief wasn't too obvious. She set the tray on the table and poured him a cup of coffee. When she handed it to him, the tips of their fingers touched. Her eyes flew to his, and he looked up at her at the same time.

"Sit down, Shay," he said softly.

Not even thinking to argue, entranced and bewildered by the emotions rioting inside her, she sank into the opposite chair. Her eyes remained riveted on his.

"Do you want some coffee?" he asked.

Shaking her head, she said almost soundlessly, "No, I don't think so."

He looked down into his cup, but she didn't think he was really seeing it. She had the distinct impression that he was gathering his thoughts, outlining what he was about to say. She stared at the top of his head, remembering the splendor of having his hair curl around her fingers. The caress had been far too brief. She longed to touch those silky black strands again.

"I know you were surprised that I came to see you today," he began.

"Yes."

"We didn't exactly part on the best of terms, did we?"

"No."

He looked up at her then, his eyes fiery. "I'm undergoing a tremendous conflict in my life, Shay."

She licked her lips. "I don't understand. What does that have to do with me?"

He grinned abashedly. "You're the conflict. It's not in keeping with what I profess, with what I am, that I continue to think of you the way I do." She thought she might suffocate from the emotion lodged in her throat. "Do you know what I'm telling you?"

She made a shrugging gesture with her shoulders that could be either affirmation or denial, but was certainly not conviction. She could barely hear his softly spoken words over the pulse drumming in her ears. She clenched clammy hands together on the tabletop.

"Your accusations were well-founded that morning after I hit you with the tennis ball. Accidentally, I hasten to add." His lips separated into a wide grin before he grew serious again. "When you accused me of enjoying touching you, you were right. I enjoyed touching you, holding you, far too much. That's why I got angry. I didn't want to admit to myself, much less to you, how holding you affected me."

"Stop," she gasped and catapulted out of her chair. "Please don't say any more." Propping herself on rigid arms, she leaned into the countertop and rested her forehead on the cabinet door. Where weeks ago she would have found this scene highly amusing and would have teased him unmercifully, now she only wanted to stop him before he said more.

She wasn't the same woman who had caught him stepping out of the shower. Something had happened to her. She hadn't been able to attach a name to it. She didn't know how to handle it.

He stood up and placed his hands on her shoulders. His touch ignited her senses, she moaned softly. "I have to tell you, don't you see? My only salvation lies in being honest about what I feel." He took a step closer. The hard strength of his body made her feel comparably weak. "Shay, that dream I was having that morning we . . . we woke up together, that was a dream I didn't want to end."

With gentle pressure on her shoulders, he turned her around to face him. Forcing her chin up with his index finger, he made her meet his eyes. His hands closed around her face. Lightly, tenderly, his thumb glided over her lips. "I didn't want it to end," he whispered.

That wonderful mouth melted onto hers, and she felt that she had come home after spending months away. For the first time in years, no, in her life, she felt whole.

His mouth slanted across hers, persuasively parting her lips. His tongue paused, hovering on the brink of great discovery before it slipped between her lips to sample the sweetness of her mouth.

She heard her own moan of pleasure echo his as her arms came around his neck. He moved closer, pressing her body between his and the countertop, both equally unyielding. His arms, hard and strong, molded her to the length of his body.

His kiss was long and deep and thoroughly sexual as his tongue dipped into the hollow of her mouth, withdrew, and probed again. "Shay, Shay," he breathed into her ear after having charted a path there with light kisses across her cheek. "I wrestled with myself as long as I could. I had to see you. I had to know if what I was feeling was real or just the aftereffects of an unusual weekend spent away from home. It had been months since I'd left Brookside for even a day. You were so different from the women my well-intentioned friends try to pawn off on me. You are so different from any woman I know."

He tilted her head back once more and, holding her jaw firmly between his fingers, kissed her with a passion that stole her breath and her reason away. "All weekend, from the moment I took that towel off my head and saw you standing there with that devilish grin on your beautiful face, I didn't know which I'd rather do, spank the daylights out of you or kiss you."

She grappled with his hands in order to bury her face in his shirtfront, to inhale the scent that belonged uniquely to him. "Me, too. I wanted to kill you one minute and kiss you the next. You ignored me. I couldn't tolerate that. Half the time you acted as if I wasn't even in the same room."

His chuckle rumbled in his ear. "Oh, I knew. I was biting imaginary bullets to keep my eyes and hands off you."

She lifted her head to weigh the measure of truth in his eyes. "And my portfolio. You analyzed the pictures aesthetically. You didn't even notice me."

His eyes, burning with an internal light, dropped to her breasts. "I noticed . . . everything. More than I should have."

He kissed her again, applying a sweet suction to her mouth, as though he wanted to draw all of her into himself. His hands roamed over her back with caressing motions. One slipped beyond her waist to cup her full hip. "Did you have a bruise?" he asked.

She smiled against his mouth, though they didn't pull away from each other. "About the size of a tennis ball. First it was royal purple, then it faded to a mute blue. Green set in next, and then it turned a sickly shade of yellow."

"I'm sorry," he said, rubbing the spot gently.

"I'm not. It proved that you're human."

"I'm all too human," he said with a growl, devouring her mouth with unleashed hunger. Not only his lips and tongue testified to his human nature, but also the steel evidence of his desire that pressed against her. She welcomed and responded to both, opening her mouth to his delicious ravishment and moving with reciprocal need against his aroused manhood.

When he pushed away at last, his chest heaving and his face flushed, he choked out, "We'd better talk." Taking her hand, he pulled her into the living room. Her feet seemed disinclined to move. His last kiss had drained her, leaving her with a debilitating lethargy. Conversely, her whole body was quivering with new-found life.

They settled close together on the couch. He took both her hands and held them on his knee. "Your mother told me you weren't involved with anyone. I want us to start seeing each other regularly, be together often. I thought we—"

She yanked her hands away as his words cooled her fevered senses like an icy bath. "Wait a minute. Back up. You asked my mother about me? About my love interests?" She trembled with anger.

For a moment he seemed stunned by her abrupt

change of mood, then he answered levelly, "No, not directly. We were talking about you one day, and she expressed her regret that you weren't married, didn't have a family, and lived alone. I asked her if you'd been . . . involved . . . with anyone since your husband, and she told me no."

"What were you doing?" Shay asked, rising to her feet. She made a beeline to the plants in the bay window, where she viciously pinched off a dead leaf. "Checking up on me to see if I was good enough to be seen with you, the holy pastor of Brookside?"

"Now, Shay," he said tightly, also coming to his feet and planting both hands on his hips, "don't fly off the handle and lose your temper."

"I'll lose my temper if I damn well please. And you would too if someone were sneaking around, snooping into your private affairs."

"I wasn't sneaking," he denied. "I was having a conversation with your mother. She brought you into it, I didn't. Why are you getting so upset? There weren't any affairs for me to find out about."

"But if there had been, what then?" she fired back. "What if she'd told you I'd had a horde of lovers since the day my divorce to Anson became final? Would you have come here today pouring out your pretty poetic speeches and kissing me?"

He ran an agitated hand through his hair as he made an attempt to control his own rising temper. "I have the same drives and needs of any man. I'm attracted to you. I *want* you. I've confessed that to myself, to you, to God."

He went to stand in the other window. She stared out sightlessly. The sun was beginning to set. A dog barked. "I'm trying to be totally honest with you," Ian said. "I'm a man, Shay. But I'm also a minister. I take my commitment to God very seriously. Everything I do, every decision of my life, has to revolve around that."

She had no argument for such an avowal, and her furious bearing slumped in defeat. She turned her back to him and absently picked up a brass atomizer to mist a fern. "Then why did you come here? The situation is hopeless. I am what I am, and you are what you are."

She heard his heels on the hardwood floor only a moment before he lifted the mister from her hand. He set it on a black wrought-iron shelf nearby and turned her to face him. "If I thought it was hopeless, I wouldn't be here. I've known nothing but torment since I saw you last. The only way I could cope with myself and the fantasies I was having was to come here and lay all my cards on the table. I, probably more than you, realize that it won't be easy. Nothing may come of it. We might part as mortal enemies or great buddies or unfulfilled lovers, but I have to find out, Shay. We owe it to ourselves to see what happens, don't you think?"

"I don't know," she said with a groan. "Ian, you're a minister. A *minister*. In all my wildest imaginings, I never thought of being involved with a clergyman."

His teeth shone whitely when he smiled. "Believe me, I never imagined myself courting a nude model either." His grin softened and faded until his countenance grew serious again. "How do you feel about spiritual matters, Shay?"

The quiet intensity of the question told her how important her answer would be to him. "I was raised a Protestant. Mom and Dad and I attended church every Sunday when I was growing up, more because Mom wanted to go than Dad. I think he felt as I do, that it's not the organization that's important but what one feels inside that counts, an individual's personal relationship with God. Anson forced me to attend services with him. I went, but rebelliously. He attended to see and be seen, not for any spiritual uplifting. I abhor that kind of hypocrisy."

"So do I. We probably have more in common than you think."

He was trying for a lighter mood, but she was still concerned. Uppermost in her mind was the thought that she might be hurt again. She had married a man who had wanted to change her. She had made him unhappy because she obviously wasn't what he had really wanted. The wounds he had inflicted on her spirit had been slow to heal. He had made her feel unworthy, shameful. And if she'd been made to feel that way by a social climber like Anson, how would she fare with a spiritual man like Ian? Dismally.

"I couldn't change, Ian. I wouldn't if I could. I prefer to think freely, to form my own opinions about things, and to voice those opinions when and where I feel like it. I'd never want to cause you embarrassment or shame, but I couldn't be stifled."

"I knew all that when I came to see you today. I like you as you are, or I wouldn't be here. As I said earlier, you're a far cry from the women who are usually pawned off on me."

"Do you have blind dates arranged for you by socalled friends?"

"When I don't adamantly refuse them. You know, so-and-so's cousin who's visiting from Iowa, or so-and-so's kid sister who just graduated from an all-girl school and has a 'very good personality.' "

Laughter took away her worried expression. "I think we have the same friends!"

He pulled her to him, and they rocked from side to side as they laughed. She wondered how she had spent the whole weekend with him yet never realized how much fun they could have together.

"Neil Diamond and Barbra Streisand are going to be at Madison Square Garden next Friday night," Ian said. "Would you meet me in the city for dinner and the concert?"

"You like Neil Diamond, too? Along with Blondie and the Bee Gees?"

"Don't forget the Beach Boys," he murmured, nuzzling her neck.

"I'll never forget the Beach Boys." She sighed as his mouth closed over hers. His tongue sought out the vulnerable spots in her mouth and stroked them. He was an inordinately talented kisser, and Shay meant to ask him how he had acquired such a technique, but he was asking his own question.

"Will you meet me? Those tickets were expensive, and I live on a minister's salary, don't forget."

She struggled to back away from him. "Are you sure you want to pursue this, Ian? I won't hold it against you if you want to shake hands and part friends now." She might die, but she wouldn't hold it against him.

"I want to do more than shake hands with you." The kisses he was planting on the side of her neck confirmed that.

It was incomprehensible to her how his mouth could so effortlessly convince her that what they were about to do was wise. "I'll meet you," she heard herself half-whimper, half-sigh.

"Penn Station? Six o'clock? Will you have any trouble getting a train?"

"Penn Station at six will be fine, but I'll drive. I don't want to take the train home late alone."

"Good idea."

More exquisite kissing followed. Finally Ian raised his head and placed his hands on her shoulders. "I've got to go so you can get your dinner."

"I could fix something for both of us," she said hopefully, swaying toward him.

He shook his head. "We've got to take this slowly. An invitation to coffee was the only way I could see to get you out of the shop and alone. I can't tell you how glad I am that there's a scarcity of coffee shops in this town."

"Absolves you of guilt?" she teased.

He grinned. "Something like that."

Still holding her hand, he hooked his sportcoat over his shoulder and went to the door. "Till Friday?"

She nodded. "Till Friday."

They stood very close, the tips of her breasts lightly grazing his shirtfront. Long ago she'd given up trying not to look at him, to pretend indifference. Having survived the weeks of loneliness since their first meeting, she feasted her eyes on him, as he did on her.

She watched, mesmerized, when his fingers came up and untied her bow tie. She felt the fabric first tightening then relaxing around her neck, or she might have thought she was imagining the whole thing. The first button on her blouse fell free. The second. She held her breath. She wouldn't stop him, no matter what he did, but she couldn't believe this was happening.

He went only as far as the third button. With heart-stopping slowness, he carefully parted her blouse. His hand slid around the column of her throat. He pressed his thumb against the pulse point at its base. It was beating erratically. "I had to touch you with some degree of intimacy." He sighed. She closed her eyes just as his mouth fused with hers.

The kiss was hot, wet, and turbulent, evoking the very act of love. His thumb kept up that hypnotic massage along her neck. It was only a suggestion of the things she wanted him to do. It was only a suggestion of the things his eyes had told her he wanted to do. He could well have been caressing her nipples for their hard contraction against his chest. His answering groan as she pressed closer told her his thoughts were running along similar lines.

The forbiddenness of such thoughts, the forced suppression of the passion they shared, only heightened the sexuality of their kiss. Deep inside, the core of her femininity exploded with sensations that rose into her chest, setting her breasts afire and making her heart swell with what felt like love. Rationally, she knew that such a possibility was both electrifying and insane, but the desire that rushed through her veins diffused its message.

Ian didn't speak again, only withdrew his hand from around her neck, regret written on his handsome face. He shut the door softly behind him.

She listened to his footsteps receding down the hallway and wondered mournfully how she was going to survive until Friday.

Chapter Six

Somehow she did survive, though during the following days she was absentminded at work, going through the motions but lacking any interest in her customers. Every time the bell on the door jingled, her eyes flew toward it in the hope that he had come to see her. If he were finding it as difficult to keep his mind on his work as she was, his arrival wouldn't be too farfetched a possibility.

Vandiveer noticed her lackadaisical attitude. "That woman would have bought that vase if you'd cared enough to talk her into it," he chastised when an indecisive customer left the shop. "Snap out of it, Shay, or go home and sleep it off. You're useless to me here walking around like a zombie."

"I'm sorry." She sighed. "I . . . I haven't been feeling well the last few days."

Vandiveer coughed behind his hand. "If I didn't know better, I'd think you were in love." Her head snapped to attention. "Well, well, well." He laughed.

"Have I struck a nerve? New beau, Shay?" His tone was silky and taunting. He'd asked her this question many times over the years she'd worked for him, with the salacious curiosity of an old maid. Her answer had always been an unqualified no.

"Possibly," she said blithely, taking up a newly framed lithograph and trying it in several display positions on the wall. "He's a minister." The days since Ian's departure from her door had been dreary enough. She might as well have some fun at old Vandiveer's expense.

She got the astonished reaction from him she had anticipated. "A minister!"

"Yes, a minister. Like in church. Have you ever been to a church, Mr. Vandiveer?"

"Once. When my mother had me christened. And then I didn't have anything to say about it." Shay chuckled. "I must admit my image of clergymen run along the lines of Bing Crosby in *Going My Way*. Where in the world did you ever meet a minister? In church?" he asked cattily.

"No," Shay replied vaguely. "No . . . uh . . . somewhere else." This was only for fun, after all. She wasn't going to divulge the ins and outs of her private life to Vandiveer. Tiring of the game and more than a little piqued by her employer's lewdly cunning expression, she added, "I know that last customer's house. I helped her with a wall arrangement. If I choose some silk flowers to match her living room and call her, she may come buy the vase."

Vandiveer seemed mollified, but at the moment Shay couldn't have cared less. Her thoughts had already gravitated back to where they had been all week—on Ian.

If her days seemed long, her nights seemed endless. As she had feared, once Ian had been in her tiny apartment, it had undergone a metamorphosis. It now seemed mammoth and hollow. She roamed the rooms, searching out projects, anything to occupy her mind with something else besides Ian.

She was obsessed with him. She saw him standing in the window, his face serious and grave. She saw him sitting on her sofa, his expression earnest and intense. She saw him lounging in the chair at her kitchen table, his long legs stretched out in front of him. He was everywhere, but he wasn't *there*. And more than she wanted to admit, she wanted him to be with her.

Before their troubles began, she and Anson had enjoyed a healthy and active sexual relationship. Their lovemaking had been frequent and lusty. But it had been the lovemaking of two children suddenly granted the privilege. It had been rowdy and playful, frequently hurried, and a trifle selfish for both of them.

Ian's passionate kisses bothered her in shocking, wonderful ways. She sensed that beneath his austere bearing there beat the heart of a fierce and tender lover. It was an exciting prospect, but one she mustn't dwell on. She might be crushingly disappointed if they ever overcame their differences and actually became lovers.

But she was wasting her time speculating on what kind of lover Ian would be. Much as she wanted to deny it, she knew the situation was impossible. She was convinced of his dedication to his calling. Had he not been so dedicated, he couldn't have left the other night with their desires unsatisfied.

Dead end. She'd never had an affair. Ian Douglas was the one man who could interest her in one. That they shared a sexual attraction was undeniable. But he wouldn't compromise his convictions. He would stand firm on all matters relating to morality. He wouldn't sleep with a woman unless he were married to her.

That was an absurd notion!

So, why is your heart pounding and why are your palms perspiring? she asked herself as she negotiated the choking Friday afternoon traffic into Manhattan. Why did you ever agree to meet him in the first place? She remembered their last kiss at the door of her apartment and knew that hell or high water couldn't have kept her from seeing him tonight.

She was thankful that most everyone else was leaving the city, heading in the opposite direction. Still, by the time she found a parking garage and walked down Seventh Avenue toward Penn Station, she felt as if she'd run a long race. The train station was like a macabre carnival, with harried commuters pushing and shoving to make their trains.

She saw Ian before he saw her. He was standing in front of the newsstand where they had agreed to meet, his eyes scanning the crowd. Shay was pleased and proud that he didn't go unnoticed by the women rushing by. More than a few turned their heads for another look after they had passed him.

They would be fools not to. He was dressed in a sportscoat and tie. His shirt was baby blue and enhanced the brilliance of his eyes. His black trousers were impeccably tailored to his muscled thighs. As always, his hair was carelessly, irresistibly disarrayed.

Moistening her dry lips, Shay walked into his field of vision. His searching eyes darted past her, skidded to a stop, and sprang back as though on an elastic band. He drank in the sight of her. When he smiled, his face lit up with warmth and happiness. Three long strides brought him to her. Closing his fingers around her elbow, he moved her against the wall out of the flow of traffic.

"Hi," he said. "You made it."

"Am I late?"

"I was early," he confessed.

For a long minute they didn't say any more, only indulged their selfish eyes by gazing at each other.

"You look beautiful," he said at last.

Her challis dress was a soft gold, a perfect color and weight for the transition into the fall season. She'd chosen it to accent the wheat color of her hair and her warm skin tones. The fabric made velvety mysteries out of her eyes as she looked up at the man staring so greedily down at her.

"Thank you."

He seemed to pull himself physically out of the beckoning depths of those eyes and brought forth a magazine he'd been holding. It was a copy of *Glamour*. "I saw a model in this and wondered if it was you."

He opened the magazine to an earmarked page. On it was an ad for a soap and sponge combination imported from France that promised to smooth away unsightly cellulite when used daily. It featured a woman in a shower. It was a three-quarter shot of the woman's back. One raised arm revealed the sloping curve of a breast. It was a black and white photograph, but the woman's hair was pulled into a loose topknot as Shay often wore hers.

"No," she said, shaking her head. She looked up at him, then across to the newsstand where he'd obviously purchased the magazine. "Have you been looking for pictures of me?" she asked, her eyes swinging back to him.

"No, no," he hastened to assure her. "I was just thumbing through this while I was waiting for you, and I thought I recognized . . . I mean it resembled your . . . uh . . . back. Are you hungry?"

He spliced the two sentences together, obviously hoping Shay would forget the first and hear only the second. She was merciful, though she had a strong desire to ask him what about the picture had looked familiar. "Yes. I haven't eaten all day."

"Celia wouldn't like that."

"Promise you won't tell her."

"Only if you'll agree to eat in one of my favorite Italian restaurants. It's only two blocks from here."

"Do they have crusty bread and fettuccine Alfredo?" She tilted her head at a charming angle.

"Gobs of both."

She linked her arm in his. "Lead the way."

They were greeted at the door of a small family-owned restaurant by a short, rotund, balding man who smothered Ian in a hearty embrace. "My friend!" he boomed, thumping Ian on the back. "You honor my restaurant after too long a time."

"Hello, Lou," Ian said, disengaging himself from the bear hug. "I'd like you to meet Shay Morrison. Shay, Luigi Pettrocelli."

Lou inspected her with dancing black eyes. "A temptation for the pastor, hey?" His elbow dug into Ian's stomach as he laughed boisterously.

"Protestants learn to cope with temptation just as our Catholic counterparts do," Ian intoned solemnly, though his lips twitched with amusement.

"Pah!" Lou turned to Shay and whispered conspiratorially, "He's been trying to convert me for years."

"And you're a hopeless case," Ian said, finally giving vent to his laughter. "Do you have anything worth eating in the kitchen tonight?"

With a flourish Lou led them to a table and rattled off a string of orders in Italian to some unseen subordinate in the kitchen. A straw-covered bottle of Chianti and a basket of breadsticks were immediately hustled out by an aproned waiter, who seemed anxious to do his boss's bidding.

"I must leave, my friend," Lou said regretfully after he'd seen to their order. "My Tony is playing soccer tonight." He reached for Shay's hand and brought it to his lips. "You are a beautiful lady and just what this stuffy Protestant needs to stir his sluggish blood."

"Tell all the kids hello and kiss Angela for me," Ian said.

"Pah! She would swoon, and I don't want her lamenting over you when she crawls into my bed!" He thumped Ian's back with a blow that might have injured a weaker man. "It is good to see you, my friend. You are always in our prayers."

"As you are in mine," Ian said, standing to embrace the other man.

Lou bowed to Shay before he waddled off toward the back of the restaurant, issuing instructions in Italian that she interpreted to be for attentive service for his friend and his lady.

"He's wonderful," she said. "I gather you've been friends for a long time. Where did you meet him?"

"On the subway." At her astounded look, he chuckled. "I was about to be mugged by three toughs late one night. Lou came bounding up behind them like a linebacker, roaring like a lion. He banged the heads of two of them together and knocked them senseless. The third one ran away."

She was laughing. "Is that the truth?"

"Every word." He crisscrossed his heart with his index finger.

"You have a very ecumenical attitude toward each other," she said, teasing.

He was smiling but serious when he answered. "We understand each other. We worship the same Lord. Men all over the world call God by different names and worship Him differently than I do. He loves us all."

Tears glistened in her eyes as she regarded him

across the candlelit table, admiring the man he was and all he stood for.

Later, as she popped the last bite of liberally buttered bread into her mouth, Ian said with amusement, "You only eat one meal a day, but it more than makes up for the other two." He inclined his head toward the platter she'd emptied.

She propped her elbows on the small, intimate table and glared at him. "Are you poking fun at my healthy appreciation of food?"

"Didn't your mother ever tell you that it's not ladylike to clean your plate? Especially in front of a suitor."

"My mother warned me about *all* the nasty things that can befall an incautious young lady."

He took a sip of Chianti and nodded to the waiter, who took away their plates. "Like what? What pitfalls did she warn you about?" Ian asked.

Shay ticked them off on her fingers, thoroughly enjoying herself. "Talking to strangers, accepting rides from men I don't know, letting a stranger into the house. Things like that."

Replete with good food and two glasses of wine—her limit since the night she'd climbed imprudently into Ian's bed—she sat back in her chair and gazed at him across the table. The friendly clatter of dishes in the kitchen, the murmur of conversation from other diners, the soft music from the overhead speakers all faded away. At that moment her world consisted only of the two of them. "The one thing she didn't warn me about," she continued, "was ministers with sexy blue eyes."

He set his wineglass aside and leaned across the table, as close to her as he could get. His eyes roved hungrily over her face. "Do you think they're sexy?" he asked, obviously pleased.

"Uh-huh."

"Why should your mother have warned you about such a thing?"

She was jolted out of her pleasant daze and back into the world of reality. "Because . . . because any feelings I might develop for such a man would confuse me."

"Why?"

She ignored his question and asked the one that had plagued her for days. "Ian, why did you become a minister?"

He signaled for coffee. The waiter obliged. After a thoughtful sip, he began. "After I graduated from Columbia, I joined the Peace Corps. It began as a lark, a frivolous whim. I had graduated with a degree in business. My father hoped I'd take over his business, but I stalled, unconvinced that was what I wanted to do with my life. The Peace Corps was a way of buying time without looking lazy or unambitious." He grinned, and even in the dim lighting his teeth shone. The candles on the table were mirrored in his eyes.

"I went to South America for two years. Without boring you with the details, I can say that my outlook on life changed while I was there. We, or I should stress *I*, had always taken my standard of living for granted. Food, warmth, and medicine if I was sick were elemental things to me but luxuries to so many other people. The hopelessness of the people affected me most of all.

"I came back filled with a zeal to be a foreign missionary. I attended seminary. It was exciting to me, Shay. For the first time I felt I really knew what I wanted to do with my life. But I had a terrible time with languages. I had learned enough conversational Spanish to get by in South America, but as for reading and writing it properly, I was unteachable. I agonized for months. Why had God filled me with such a determination to do something, only to make it impossible for me to accomplish it?"

Without thinking, Shay covered his fingers with hers. He turned his hand over and captured hers, squeezing lightly. "One day while I was still in the seminary, a friend of my mother's came to me in tears, crying for her husband who was an alcoholic. We prayed together. I counseled her and finally managed to see the husband and talk to him. After several such occasions, when I was able to help the people I related to, it occurred to me that God was trying to tell me something."

Ian seemed embarrassed by his simplistic explanation. "You don't have to go halfway around the world to find suffering and need," he went on. "My congregation may have more amenities than their counterparts in an Indian village in South America can imagine, but spiritual deficiency is universal. It knows no boundaries—not geographical, not social, not economical." His eyes begged for her understanding. "Have I answered your question?"

She nodded without speaking. Yes, he had answered her question. She understood him better now and was faced with a bleak truth. She, Shay Morrison, had no calling like Ian did. She could share nothing of his life. She couldn't be even a small part of it.

Ian consulted his watch and winced. "Can you forgo dessert until after the concert? If we don't hurry, Neil and Barbra will start without us."

They arrived just in time, plopping breathlessly into their seats after dashing down two blocks.

The concert was excellent. They applauded when encouraged to, laughing from the sheer pleasure they derived from the music. More than once Ian brought his fingers to his lips and piercingly whistled his approval of the performers.

Catching her wide, dismayed eyes on him, he

leaned down and shouted in her ear over the roar of the crowd, "Don't look so shocked. I don't do that from the pulpit." He winked at her and threw an arm around her shoulders, hugging her tight.

During the poignant ballads, he held her hand, stroking her palm with his thumb. After one song with particularly romantic lyrics, the spotlight gradually faded to black. Ian reached over, threaded his fingers through her hair, and turned her toward him. Their mouths found each other in the total darkness.

His tongue barely breached her lips to touch the tip of hers, but she felt its caress deep inside her. Pinpricks of desire between her thighs brought a soft moan to her lips, a moan he captured with his mouth. Her breasts swelled with awakening passion. Her nipples tingled with expectation.

She knew then that what she'd felt with Anson had been the sensual enlightenment of a curious youth not far from her teens. What she felt for Ian was the strong, passionate drive of a woman, mature, full of need, wanting to share her body with a man who felt the same instinctive compulsion to be made complete by joining with another.

They left Madison Square Garden absorbed by the throng. Shay didn't mind the crowd. She actually welcomed the press. It gave her an excuse to keep her body plastered to Ian's. As she walked before him, her buttocks fit snugly against him. To prevent them from getting separated, he locked his arms around her waist.

Occasionally his biceps bumped into the sides of her breasts. Since she wore only a lacy camisole under her dress, those accidental touches induced erotic fantasies she was certain would have shocked her escort. But when she glanced up at him over her shoulder, laying her head against his chest to do so, the look in his eyes told her he could well be sharing and participating in her fantasies.

The place he'd selected to take her for dessert was a restaurant famous for its pastries and operatic memorabilia. It was a bustling narrow restaurant with patrons and waiters calling out orders piped in arias. Ian managed to squeeze them into a table and shout their order to a rushing waiter. Miraculously, within minutes they were being served pastries and aromatic coffee.

"What is this high caloric monstrosity?" Shay asked, probing with her fork at the base of a culinary sculpture.

"Just eat it," Ian commanded. He watched with delight as she dug into the layers of pastry, chocolate mousse, whipped cream, and slivered almonds. She'd bemoan any residual bulges later. For the time being she was unrepentantly gluttonous.

As they were leaving the noisy nightspot, a man entering the door Ian was holding whirled around and cried, "Shay! Is that you, my darling Shay? It is! How are you, darling?"

He leaned toward her and, bobbing his head forward, kissed first one of her cheeks then the other in an affected manner.

"Hello, Armand," she said flatly.

"It's been ages and ages," he gushed.

"Yes, it has," she agreed, thinking that it hadn't been long enough and that it would be another long time if she had anything to do about it.

The man's reptilian eyes appraised Ian, and apparently approving, he smiled up at him. "Armand Boliver, my friend Ian Douglas," Shay said, executing the introduction emotionlessly.

"Charmed," the man said, offering a limp hand to Ian, who shook it very briefly. "Working much, Shay?" Armand asked, keeping his eyes on Ian.

"Now and then."

"You're too modest, darling. I heard you're going to pose for Robert Glad starting next week. He does absolutely divine things in wood—if he doesn't get carried away with his chisel."

The remark was intentionally snide and laden with sexual innuendo, but Shay chose to disregard both. She couldn't lie and say it had been nice to see Armand. Instead she excused them by saying, "It's late. Good night, Armand."

Without giving the man a chance to speak, she

grabbed Ian's arm and pulled him away. He didn't seem inclined to linger either. For several blocks they walked in tense silence. Shay knew Ian was curious, but she wasn't going to explain unless he asked. As they waited for a traffic light to change, he turned to her. "Have you ever—"

"No!" she said, shaking her head adamantly. "I've never posed for him."

They crossed the street before Ian pursued the topic. "What does he do?"

"He's a photographer," she said crisply. "A sorry excuse for one, if you ask me. My agent sent me to him on a go-see. I stayed in his studio—and I use the term loosely; pleasure palace would be far more appropriate—for exactly two minutes. I've never gone back. Nor will I. I've heard all kinds of tales since then about what goes on in that room lined with leopard skin. Drugs, orgies." She shuddered. "He gives me the creeps, and he's never forgiven me for laughing when he suggested that I take off all my clothes and lie down on his vibrating waterbed."

She stopped in her tracks as Ian issued a blistering curse through his teeth. He grasped her arm and spun her around. "If he hurt you—"

"No," she said firmly. The feral light in Ian's eyes alarmed her. To the passionate nature she sensed in Ian she added a volatile temper. But then she'd seen evidences of it before, just not to this degree. If she'd given the least hint that Armand had done something unpleasant to her, she felt certain Ian would have gladly gone back and leveled the man. "Armand is too much of a coward to hurt anyone," she added. "Did you hear what he said about Robert Glad? That's just the kind of petty remark I'd expect him to make about someone with real talent."

"Who's Robert Glad?"

"He's a sculptor who works mainly in wood." They were touching upon a sensitive subject, and she wished she could think of an unobtrusive way to change it.

"That . . . that Armand person said you were posing for Glad. Next week."

"Yes."

After another lengthy, awkward silence, Ian picked up the conversation. "Will you . . . I mean, is it . . ."

She came to a sudden halt in the middle of the sidewalk and faced him. "Nude? Is that the word you find so difficult to say?"

"No. I mean, yes, that's the word, but no, I don't find it difficult to say!"

"Sure you don't," she ground out. "You were going through that magazine tonight before I got there looking for pictures of me, like a temperance marcher sniffing out demon liquor."

"Shay—"

"Is Armand the kind of artist you picture me work-

ing for? That base, decadent worm?" She pulled herself up to her full height and tossed her head back
proudly. "For your information, I'm as particular
about the artists I'll work with as they are in choosing
me. And to satisfy your curiosity, so you won't be too
embarrassed to ask again, yes, my breasts will be bare
next week, though the rest of me will be covered.
Robert Glad, a famous sculptor, has been commissioned by a historical society in Hawaii to do a piece
for a museum. He's using a Polynesian girl's face but
my torso. Now, does all that meet with your moralistic
approval?"

"You're not being fair, Shay," Ian said with a calm-
ness that further infuriated her.

"Nor are you." Her body was taut with anger.
Every muscle was straining with it. "You formed an
opinion about me when you caught me looking at you
naked. All right, that was a dreadful sin. Gouge out
my eyes. Start the fires at the stake."

He, too, was getting angry. Several passersby stared
at them, but they were hardly aware of anything except their anger and their problem, which at the moment seemed insurmountable. The hopelessness of it
contributed to Shay's fury.

"You have a beautiful body, Reverend Douglas. I
have a deep, artistic appreciation for beautiful bodies,
so I looked at you. And yes, I liked what I saw. And

no, I wasn't looking strictly aesthetically. And damn it, I wish I didn't still want you."

She spun away from him, only to collide with the side of a newsstand. She scanned the lurid display with tear-filled eyes, and her stomach turned in revulsion. The selection of magazines varied only in their degree of tastelessness. All the reading matter was pornographic. Choking on her hurt and anger, she turned back to Ian. "Why don't you buy some of these and pore over them carefully to see if I'm in them? That's what you liken me to, isn't it?" Her hand swept the rack, knocking a number of the magazines to the sidewalk.

The proprietor came off his stool and shouted at her, "Hey, lady, what the hell do you think you're doin'?"

She stumbled blindly down the sidewalk, then turned to see Ian shove a five-dollar bill at the man, who was cursing them both viciously with each chomp on his stale, unlit cigar. She glimpsed Ian rushing after her and heard him calling her name as she entered the parking garage and gave her license number to the attendant.

Just as the man disappeared to get the car, Ian caught up with her. He yanked her around, catching a wrist in each of his fists. He pressed his body into hers to still her attempt to escape.

"You know better, Shay, you know better," he said.

The words came out in breathless gasps. He pressed closer to her, buried his face in her hair, and repeated the words again and again until she grew calm and her body sank against him in submission.

His arms went around her, and they clung to each other in the gloomy, echoing cavern of the garage, mindless of the danger they were foolishly courting.

When he raised his head, he smoothed back her hair with both hands. "You're wrong. I don't think of you as anything but what you are, a beautiful woman. I know what you do. I *do*. Here"—he thumped the side of his head with the heel of his hand—"I can accept it. It's here"—he placed his hand over his heart—"that I can't."

He burrowed his nose into the side of her neck. "I don't like what you do. I admit it. Not for the reasons you think, but because I can't bear the thought of slime like Armand, or any man, *any* man, having the opportunity to look at what I crave to look at so much, what I crave to touch, to taste."

She uttered a short, joyful cry and turned her mouth toward his. "Ah, Shay, Shay," he breathed before he sealed their mouths together in a timeless kiss.

The air left his lungs and gushed into her mouth. She swallowed it greedily. Her arms lifted and closed around his neck as her head went back to allow him greater access to her mouth. He was voracious, roughly varying the angles of their lips, plunging deeply into the sweet crevice of her mouth with a debauching tongue.

She wove her fingers in his hair, pulling him closer, tasting him and loving the taste, loving the texture of his mouth. There had always been a part of herself she had held inviolate. Neither her parents nor Anson nor anyone else had ever touched that secret part of her that was her soul. She had kept that in reserve. Now she opened it up and offered it freely to Ian, making it his for the taking.

When his initial appetite had been appeased, he sipped at her mouth tenderly and let his tongue glide leisurely over lips that were swollen from the passion of their kisses.

"You taste the way you look," he whispered hoarsely. "Warm and sweet and golden."

His hands caressed her. Their strength gave her a sheltered, protected feeling that she basked in. She'd been alone for too long. She reveled in being treated like a prized treasure belonging to someone special.

"I can't get enough," he said in anguish as he took her mouth again.

He was a man of God; she had no doubt of that. But from the way their bodies were moving against each other as his legs straddled hers, she knew, too, that he was of the generations of Adam. He was a man. And everything in her that was woman cried out for him.

Tentatively his hand crept up her ribs. She held her

breath, then expelled it on a long, shuddering sigh when the tips of his fingers stroked the under-curve of her breast, back and forth, twice, three times, while her mind went spinning out in space and her heart leapt within that which he touched so softly.

He lifted his hand until it hovered over her nipple, which was hard with yearning. For endless seconds he kept his hand suspended over her, and she heard his breathing entering and leaving his lungs, felt it warm on her neck.

"Shay," he said in a strangled voice. He dropped one hand to his side, but pulled her tighter with his other across the middle of her back. He nestled his face in the warm hollow between her neck and shoulder.

She suppressed an impulse to scream in frustration. Instead, as the attendant drove her car around a corner, pulled to a stop, and got out, she disengaged herself from Ian's arms, opened the car door, and slid inside.

"Shay—"

She slammed the door shut but rolled down the window to say, "I told you this wasn't going to work. It's impossible."

Leaning down with his arms braced against the car, he squeezed his eyes shut and shook his head. "No," he rasped. "No, it's not."

Quickly he brushed a kiss across her forehead. Straightening, he said, "Drive carefully."

Chapter Seven

*I*t was over. She knew it. From the moment she drove out of the parking garage and left him standing alone in the shadows, staring grimly after her, she knew that her love of Ian Douglas was a lost cause. It always had been. She'd only been fooling herself to think otherwise. Her passionate nature had been buoyed by his caresses. He couldn't have been unaware of it. Nor could his moral code fail to feel threatened by it.

Why hadn't she resisted? Or why hadn't she feigned indignation and slapped his face? Or why hadn't she taken his hand away and kissed it sympathetically, softly suggesting that they shouldn't play with fire? Why hadn't she done *something*, anything except return his kisses and caresses with such wanton eagerness?

No doubt he now saw her as an instrument of the Devil sent to tempt him into jeopardizing his career and all he stood for.

When she didn't hear from him by the end of the second week, she knew that he was trying to expunge her from his soul. He couldn't have misinterpreted the language her body had spoken to his. She had wanted his touch. She had wanted it all over her. Arms and shoulders, back and hips and breasts and thighs, and the most secret parts of her body had cried out for him in a silent demand that he must have heard. Nor had she camouflaged her frustration when he had removed his hand from her nipple that yearned for his touch. Her kiss, too, had been unrestrained and thoroughly revealing.

By the end of the third week she was asking why she should care what the provincial, stodgy minister of Brookside, Connecticut, thought of her. After all, her dalliance with him had only been an experiment, hadn't it? From the very beginning, hadn't she used him for her own amusement? The time she'd spent with him had provided her with a few hours of diversion. Now it was over. So, fine. *Fine*. She didn't care.

Besides, in addition to keeping busy with her job at the gallery, she was going into the city every third day to pose for Robert Glad. She appreciated his professionalism. His talent was remarkable and unsurpassed, although his dour personality left a lot to be desired.

Whenever she arrived at his studio, a bearded, rumpled Robert Glad ushered her in with hardly a word and indicated the back room where she should change. Emerging draped in a long sheet, she would allow him to position her and settle her into the pose she might have to hold for hours. He fussily adjusted the sarong-type garment around her waist, then he would begin, scowling as he applied his tools to the block of mahogany that was slowly taking form. When he was finished for the session, he slung the metal tools on his worktable and said a terse, "Thank you," then she changed hastily back into street clothes and left.

She didn't mind his disinclination to speak. While she stood posed before him, she felt removed from the world, temporarily relieved of responsibility, and free to let her thoughts wander.

Her mind seemed determined to dwell on Ian and their brief, tumultuous relationship, if that term was appropriate. Round and round, again and again, in ceaseless circles, she reviewed their problem. The solution always came out the same: the situation was hopeless. It always had been. It always would be. She must resign herself to that fact.

Then why was the prospect of never seeing Ian again so devastating? Why did his rejection hurt so much? From the beginning she had known their flirtation would be temporary. But it came as a surprise to her to find that life was so very bleak without him. Not nearly as great, however, as her surprise in finding him waiting for her outside Robert Glad's studio one afternoon.

Despondently, as had been her mood for the past three weeks, she had pushed through the front door, sucked out by the autumn wind that sped through the urban canyons. When she saw him pacing the sidewalk, she came to an abrupt halt. He was staring down at his feet as he painstakingly measured out his steps. He was wearing a light overcoat. The wind's disarrangement of his hair was far sexier than any hairstylist could have achieved.

He looked up and saw her as she stood there clutching her oversized bag to her chest. His pacing stopped abruptly.

"Ian?" she asked, looking back at the building she had just left to assure herself that she wasn't dreaming.

"Hi."

"How did you know where I was?"

"I followed a hunch and looked up Glad's address in the phone book. I wanted to see you. I've been waiting for over an hour."

She gathered her resolve, drew herself up straight, and marched brusquely past him. "Well, you could have spared yourself the time and effort," she said. "I've got to catch a train back to Woodville. I promised Vandiveer I'd put in a couple of hours at the shop before closing."

"Shay," he said, catching her arm and pulling her to a stop, "are you angry with me for not calling?"

The wind made a riot of her wheat-colored curls. She shook them impatiently off her face. "Don't flatter yourself." Her efforts to pull free from his grip only made him increase the pressure on her arm.

"After what happened last time, I thought it would be better if we didn't see each other for a while," he said quietly.

"And you were right. Only I think it would be better if we *never* saw each other again." She had to force the words from her throat. She wanted nothing more than to throw herself at him, to wrap her arms around the body that haunted her fantasies, to feel the heat of his mouth on hers. In the gray light of the cloudy afternoon his vivid blue eyes seemed to be the only bright thing, offering the only hope and happiness in her life. Yet they were denied her. "I know why you didn't call," she said. "You don't want to be tainted by a scarlet woman like me. I can't tell you how relieved I was when you didn't persist in seeing me. Good-bye, Ian. I'm in a hurry."

She pulled her arm away and even took a few steps before he pulled her to another jarring halt. His face was only inches above hers as he drew her against him. "I didn't call because I wanted you too much." She stared up at him wordlessly, her eyes wide, her lips parted. "Don't you understand, Shay? It was killing me to stop myself from making love to you."

She tugged on her arm to no avail. He wouldn't release it. Perversely, she was glad to know that he had suffered as much as she had, and for the same reason. That he could continue to tamper with her shattered emotions spurred her temper. "Thank you very much, Reverend Douglas, but I don't like being considered the evil influence in your life." Tears filled her eyes, which made her even more furious. She didn't want him to know how much he had hurt her. Maybe he would think the cold wind was responsible for the moisture beading her lashes.

"No, no," he said, shaking his head and gathering her to him. He opened his coat and pressed her head against the soft, warm sweater that covered his chest. His fingers threaded through her hair and settled on her scalp, holding her fast. "Neither of us is evil, Shay. Sex isn't evil. We've responded to each other as God intended two healthy adults attracted to each other should." Propping his chin on the top of her head, he enclosed her in his coat. "It's how we're going to deal with that sexual attraction that I've been deliberating about for the past three weeks. And I couldn't risk having your distracting influence close by to cloud my good judgment."

She sniffed back her tears and raised her head to look at him. "Well, I suppose being a distracting influence is better than being an evil one." She smiled shakily.

Lowering his head, he planted a tender kiss on her mouth. "I missed you."

"Did you?" She pretended coyness to keep from raising on her tiptoes and covering his face with kisses.

"Yes. I came here today to invite you personally to spend the weekend with me in Brookside."

She stared at him incredulously. "Have you lost your mind?"

He laughed and squeezed her tight. "Come on, I'll treat you to a cab ride to the train station. On the way I'll convince you that I haven't taken leave of my senses."

When they were ensconced in the lumpy backseat of the cab, he took her hand and placed it on his knee. He studied it as his thumb caressed each knuckle.

"Come to Brookside this weekend. See what it's like, what my life there is like. Come on the train Saturday morning. We'll spend the day acquainting you with the town. I want you to attend church with me Sunday morning. I'll drive you home Sunday evening."

The invitation portended more than a fun weekend. What was left unsaid far outweighed what he had spoken aloud. The question of a commitment implied in his invitation frightened her. She hedged, turning her head to gaze out the window in order to avoid his opinion-swaying good looks. "Where would I stay?"

He chuckled lightly. "Did you think I was suggesting something illicit? No. In all humility, I think that my congregation holds me in nothing but the highest regard, but I don't think any of them would approve of their pastor inviting an attractive young woman to stay the night under his bachelor roof. I'd get a room for you at the local inn."

Her mind was warring with her desire to be with him and her fear that she wouldn't fit into his world. What opinions would the people of his church form of her? Not much that was good, she was sure. "I don't think so, Ian," she said finally. "Maybe some other time."

He sighed heavily. "You've forced me to tell you the real reason behind the invitation." Alarm at his guilty tone brought her head around, but she was instantly relieved to see amusement in his eyes. "I confess to an ulterior motive. Saturday night we're having a church supper climaxed by a raffle drawing. A member of the church has donated a mink coat as the prize. I thought that a stunning woman modeling the coat would create interest and perhaps urge the gentlemen in the audience to buy more chances. That's the real reason I invited you. Would you please come and model the mink for us?"

A smile tugged at the corners of her lips as she

drew her brows together speculatively. "I don't know. What does it pay?"

Imitating her seriousness, he said, "All the clam chowder you can eat . . . and my company, of course."

"Clam chowder's not one of my favorites, but . . ." She pondered a while longer. "What are you raising money for?"

"A retirement home for aging nude models."

She lit into him with both fists flying. Laughing, he dodged them and finally managed to capture her flailing arms before she could do much damage. She was slow to be subdued, but he finally held her against him, his arms across her back barring her escape.

"I thought that'd get a reaction out of you. Actually the funds will go toward outfitting a youth center."

"You consider that to be a worthy cause?"

"Very much so." His eyes impaled her with lances of brilliant light. "Please come, Shay. I think it's important to us that you do."

Yes, it would be important to them. Could she adjust to his lifestyle? Could he bend to her free way of thinking? For some reason she didn't resent this experiment of his. She herself needed the answers to questions that had plagued her for weeks. Were there any terms on which they could come together?

While she was still mulling over her decision, they left the cab and entered Grand Central Station. He didn't press her; he gave her time and space to sort out her thoughts.

"Our parents will hear about it," she said after Ian had bought her train ticket and they were waiting in the most private spot they could find.

"I thought of that, too. How do you feel about it?"

She shrugged. "I guess they have to know sooner or later."

"Okay. We'll let them know beforehand. I certainly don't want to be furtive about it."

"No." She stared blindly at the ribbing of his sweater directly in front of her. He was waiting for her answer. When she came right down to it, all her justifications and rationalizations were just that. The heart of the matter was that she wanted to go. She wanted to be with him. The anger and resentment she had manufactured out of her hurt had dissolved the moment she'd seen him pacing outside Robert Glad's studio.

All her life she'd felt a loneliness, a separateness from other people, but she hadn't known what loneliness was until the past three weeks. If only for a little while, she wanted to believe she and Ian could belong together.

"Shay."

He whispered her name, and despite the noise and bustle around them, she heard. Lifting her face to his, she welcomed the firm pressure of his lips on hers.

His tongue slipped between them like a predator assured of the kill. Each shallow, rapid thrust sent an electrical charge missiling through her body.

"This is coercion," she said breathlessly against his throat when at last he freed her mouth.

"Can you be coerced?" he asked in a hot, fervent whisper that rushed into her ear and raised gooseflesh on her skin.

She pushed slightly away from him and looked beguilingly up at him. "I've never had a fur coat. What does one wear under a mink?"

Shay caught an early Saturday morning train. Ian was waiting at the station for her. Upright minister or not, he hugged her heartily and kissed her soundly when she stepped off the train.

The town was charming, absolutely charming. A picture of it belonged in an almanac as the stereotypical Connecticut township, Shay decided. Built around a green, the town spread out over several symmetrical blocks. Even the architecture of the commercial buildings was quaint. The colonial houses could have come out of a history book.

Driving her down the tree-lined streets, Ian proudly showed off his community. "This is the high school. Championship basketball team two years in a row. The center is a member of my church. And that's

Griffin's Hardware Store. Mr. Griffin is a deacon. You'll see the church later."

He pulled his station wagon into the driveway of a two-story colonial house set on a vast lawn colorfully littered with fallen autumn leaves. It was built of white clapboard, and hunter green shutters flanked with windows.

"Welcome to the parsonage," he said, cutting the motor and watching closely for her reaction.

"This is where you live?" she asked in disbelief. "It's beautiful." Shay hadn't known what to expect, but it hadn't been anything on so grand a scale.

He laughed. "Don't be too impressed. It's belonged to the church since before I was born. It needs a new roof, and the plumbing's contrary at best."

He came around to her door to assist her out. "Let's go inside."

A wonderful smell greeted Shay the moment Ian flung open the front door. "Mrs. Higgins?" he called.

An elderly woman hurried from one of the back rooms—Shay guessed the kitchen—wiping her hands on a towel. "Hello. Is this the young lady?" she asked without compunction.

"This is Shay Morrison, Mrs. Higgins. And, Shay, this is the only woman in my life," Ian said, placing an affectionate arm around the woman, who blushed girlishly. "She's refused my proposals of marriage, but I couldn't live without her."

"Hello, Mrs. Higgins," Shay said.

"Hello, Miss Morrison. Welcome. Don't believe a word this boy says. He's always teasing. And he's far too handsome for his own good." She looked at Ian with a scolding expression, but her eyes sparkled fondly. "Would you like coffee now? I baked some gingerbread."

"We'd love some, thank you. But Shay wants to see the house first."

"It'll be ready when you are," the woman called over her shoulder as she turned back toward the kitchen.

"She's a jewel," Shay said as Ian led her into the stately dining room. "Where did you find her?"

"At church. Her husband died right after I came here. All her children had left home and had families of their own. She was deteriorating quickly because she didn't have anyone to fuss over anymore. Her family had been her whole life. So I asked her if she'd be interested in coming in for a few hours every day to cook my meals and do light housekeeping. She was here at seven the next morning." He smiled warmly. "Sometimes I have to shoo her out the door."

"You really are a very nice man," Shay said, tilting her head to the side as though assessing him for the first time. "And Mrs. Higgins was right. You're far too handsome for your own good."

"Prove it." Taking her hand, he dragged her into a

tight space between the heavy living-room door and the wall.

"Prove what?" she asked, lightheaded and breathless at the way he anchored her against him.

"That you think I'm handsome." His mouth grazed hers, their noses bumped, their bodies molded together. "Put your arms around my neck." She obliged, using unnecessarily languid movements that caused their stomachs and hips to rub together. He groaned her name softly and buried his face in her neck. "I'm so glad you're here," he whispered.

"Prove it."

"Prove what?"

"That you're glad I'm here. Kiss me long and hard."

"My pleasure."

The tour of the house was delayed a good fifteen minutes. Mrs. Higgins was expressing worry about her gingerbread cooling off by the time they completed the tour and walked arm in arm into the kitchen, feeling flushed and short-winded. Their discomposure had nothing to do with the steep flight of stairs they'd climbed to the second story.

Shay couldn't remember a day she had enjoyed more. The weather was glorious. The sapphire sky provided a contrast to the vibrant fall colors that splashed the landscape like spilled paint on a canvas.

They ate lunch in a sandwich shop owned by a

young couple who were members of Ian's church. He took every opportunity to introduce Shay to the many people who spoke to him as he showed her the interesting landmarks of the town. He seemed proud to have her on his arm. She wasn't greeted with the suspicion or censure she had feared, but rather with hopeful curiosity. Apparently everyone in Ian's congregation was concerned about their pastor's single state and hoped he would soon remedy it.

Shay smiled a sad, secret smile. If they were counting on her to fill that void in his life, they were in for a disappointment. She didn't know what the future had in store for them, but she'd never make a minister's wife. A minister's mistress? That, too, was out of the question. Then what was she doing here?

Enjoying myself, she told herself adamantly. *No harm can come of this.* She pushed all her disturbing thoughts aside, determined not to let them cloud her pleasure in the day.

To her regret, Ian had to spend a couple of hours in the afternoon studying his sermon for the following day. "I've worked on it all week, but I need to go over my notes once more." They were on the front porch of the inn where he had secured her a room. Her bags had already been taken upstairs by the kindly man who served both as desk manager and bellman. "You don't mind being left alone for a while, do you?"

"Of course not. I had to get up early this morning. I think I'll take a nap."

"Okay. I'll be by at six-thirty. If you need anything, call the house. You won't disturb me."

"Then why are you leaving me here? Why can't I just come home with you?"

He hugged her fiercely and growled in her ear, "Because you disturb me."

The church supper was boisterous and fun. The hall behind the sanctuary was jammed with a noisy crowd of people of all ages, from old men discussing the sad state of public affairs to children darting through the adults in a perpetual game of chase. Several ladies of the church had been simmering the thick, rich chowder all day, and it made a warm, filling supper for the nippy evening.

By mid-afternoon, word had spread that Reverend Douglas was bringing a lady friend to the supper that night. Shay had entered the hall with a timidity that irritated her. At one and the same time, she longed for everyone's approval and resented the fact that she wanted it so badly. She needn't have worried. She was accepted warmly into the fold. Within half an hour she felt relaxed and joined freely in the jocularity.

When the last of the dessert cakes had been devoured, Ian brought a microphone to the small stage and asked for everyone's attention.

"We still have a lot of tickets on sale back there," he said. "Remember all proceeds go to the purchase of the old Windsor house, which will be converted into a youth center. I want to provide all you tight-fisted gentlemen with a little incentive. Shay," he called to her behind a curtain, where she was slipping on the mink jacket.

Out she came, swathed in the fur, bundled up like the cutest snow bunny ever to grace the slopes. Wolf whistles and catcalls filled the hall. The men in the audience applauded loudly, while their wives, Shay noticed, cast covetous glances at the luscious fur.

A woman with five children won the coat. All five children and the husband, who looked overworked and weary, clustered excitedly around the woman as Shay helped her try on the coat.

Afterward, Shay felt tired, but pleasantly so. They stayed behind after the hall had cleared to help the janitor clean up and rearrange the chairs for Sunday School the following morning. On their way to the car, Ian walked behind her, massaging her shoulders through her coat.

"Thanks for helping," he said as he opened the car door for her. He kissed her on the ear, an absent-minded, husbandly type kiss. The thought should have knocked Shay off her feet. Instead she was smiling contentedly as they drove through the dark streets.

"I'm glad she was the one to win it," she said as Ian headed back to the inn.

"You didn't rig it, did you?" he asked suspiciously. She had drawn the winning ticket out of the large bowl.

"I'll never tell," she said in a singsong voice as she laid her head against the seat back.

Ian pulled the car in front of the inn and cut the engine. He placed his arm along the back of the seat and turned toward her. "Should I kiss you good night on the porch?"

"How about on the lips?"

He glowered at her from beneath dark brows. "Will kissing you spare me the bad plays on words?"

"Try it."

He grinned wolfishly and reached for her, pulling her across the seat. "Come here."

His mouth was as hot as a furnace as it opened over hers. She loved its heat and begged with her ready response to be consumed by it. He opened her coat and slipped his hands inside. One went around her waist to her back. With lazy indifference that drove her mad, the other flirted with the satin shoulder strap of her bra beneath her blouse.

Her hands clutched at his head, taking up handfuls of thick dark hair. Brazen fingertips examined the texture of his earlobes and moved along his hard cheek, his stubborn jaw. Curious, she trailed her hands down past his coat and toyed with the top button on his sports shirt. When it came undone, she encountered the springy hair that covered his chest, his abdomen, his . . .

"Ian," she cried softly and pushed away from him.

"What?" he asked, startled. He withdrew his hand from her coat.

"Nothing, nothing," she mourned softly, lowering her head and replacing her hand with her lips. His chest hair was soft, the skin warm. She bathed it with the residual dew of their kiss, which still glossed her lips.

"Sweet . . . Shay . . . please." His fingers entwined in her hair, making the meaning of his request unclear.

"Ian, Ian," she whispered, brushing her lips back and forth, "I remember what you look like. Here." She paused for only a heartbeat before letting her hand sweep across the front of his trousers.

"Ahhh, Shay." It was a sharp, strangled cry from a throat tight with passion. He grabbed her audacious hand and brought it to his lips, burying his mouth in the soft flesh of her palm. "I remember you, too." His glazed eyes focused on her breasts. In the dim light she saw his eyes drop to her lap where her upper thighs arrested his gaze. "I remember all of you."

He kissed her hand once more with an aggression that bordered on savagery. Then with the anger of a man sexually thwarted, he shoved open his door and all but dragged her out of the car.

Their kiss at the door of the inn was brief, chaste, and supremely unsatisfactory.

Ian nearly laughed out loud when he picked Shay up the next morning. She looked more prim than he'd ever seen her, in a navy wool dress with a white Peter Pan collar and a neat row of red buttons down the tucked bodice.

Ian's church was lovely, traditional in design with Corinthian columns in front of wide double doors. A slender steeple with a sedate white cross at its pinnacle pointed toward heaven. But the spirit inside made the church what it was. And the man in the pulpit was partly responsible for that loving spirit.

His sermon that morning was on the subject of love. "There are no degrees of love as it is described in the Bible," he told the congregation. "Either you love or you don't. It is either totally unselfish and unconditional or it isn't real love."

Shay felt like crying as she sat in the pew looking up at his commanding form.

Mrs. Higgins cooked them a sumptuous lunch, which Ian graciously invited her to share with them. Shay knew his reason was twofold. First, Sunday was the loneliest day of the week for people who were alone. Second, they needed a chaperone.

At three o'clock they went to the high-school gym where he had arranged to meet some of the players on the basketball team for a workout. Looking as fit in his shorts and tank top as any of the men fifteen years his junior, he gave them a run for their money on the court. Shay sat in the bleachers, cheering him on. When he scored a particularly spectacular point, he turned to her and bowed, then threw her a kiss. She wanted to cry then, too.

"Say, you weren't bad, Old Man," one of the boys joked when the game was over.

Mopping perspiration from his brow with a towel, Ian eyed the boys smugly. "Yeah, and you lost your bet. Three Bible study sessions in a row without missing."

The boys groaned but promised to be there. Shay saw that he could relate to them, meet them on their level, and it was obvious that they admired and respected not only his physical prowess, which awed them, but also his character. The boys would do well to pattern themselves after Ian Douglas.

As they left the gym, Shay felt a familiar tightening in her throat.

After the conclusion of the Bible study groups that evening, they took only enough time to change clothes before they started the drive to Woodville.

"What did you think of my sermon?" Ian asked as the station wagon rolled along the highway with Sunday's late shadows slanting across its path. This was the first time all weekend he'd asked for her opinion about his work and his way of life.

"It was wonderful," Shay said emotionally.

Again she felt ridiculously close to tears without knowing why. "I liked everything—your town, your house, your church, and the people in it."

"You enjoyed yourself? You had a good time?"

Not trusting herself to speak, she nodded.

Ian's face expressed deep tenderness as he clasped his hand in hers. They drove in silence the rest of the way to her apartment.

"Brrrr," Ian said, carrying her suitcase inside. "It's cold in here. Didn't you leave on any heat when you left?"

"No. I didn't count on it getting so cold this weekend."

"Is that wood ready to light?" he asked, indicating the logs stacked on the grate.

"Even the kindling. I've been waiting for a chance to have a fire."

"No time like the present." He rubbed his hands together before dropping to his knees to check the damper.

By the time the fire was cheerily licking at the logs, she had prepared two mugs of hot chocolate. "This will ward off the chill on the inside," she said, setting the tray on the floor and plopping down beside Ian, who sat staring into the flames.

Minutes passed as they sat there silently, not touching, not even looking at each other, only gazing into the fire while the steaming chocolate cooled. It had become tepid by the time Shay tasted it. Ian turned his head and looked at her with a monumental question in his eyes.

He must have seen an answer in hers. Wordlessly, he moved aside the tray. They came to each other as though a pair of benevolent hands had granted their most heartfelt wish and pushed them together.

Their mouths formed an inseparable bond as Ian lowered them to the rug. As though this coming together were predestined, they adjusted their bodies to each other. Their legs became sandwiched. Their arms competed to gain the most ground. Her soft breasts cushioned his hard chest.

"You're so beautiful . . . beautiful." Shay gasped in surprise when his tongue found the delicate interior of her ear. "Your skin feels so good against my mouth."

His lips found hers once again as he rolled them over until she was lying on top of him. His head came off the floor to take tiny love bites out of her neck while his hands plunged beneath her cotton knit sweater and caressed the silky warmth of her back.

His fingers coasted down her ribs. His palms barely brushed the sides of her breasts, but it was enough to make them both murmur with longing. With his hands still under her sweater, he rolled them over again. This time he lay on top of her in a timeless embrace.

His eyes drilled into hers as his hand closed gently around her bare breast. "I've relived that morning last summer a million times," he confessed hoarsely. "I thought I was dreaming, but maybe I wasn't. Maybe that was just the excuse I invented for touching you like this. I had wanted to touch you since I first saw you. You feel as beautiful as you are, Shay."

"I was dying for you to touch me," she whispered. "Touch me now." She clasped his head between her palms and brought his mouth down to hers. His fingers fanned the aroused peak of her breast as her tongue brazenly rubbed the tip of his.

Eager to know the feel of his skin, she raised his sweater to bare his stomach. Desire took her beyond inhibition as her fingers combed through the crinkly hair and found the spot where the growth pattern began to narrow and the texture became silky. She followed it to the fly of his jeans.

He drew in a shuddering breath, but she didn't need that sound to alert her to his arousal, which throbbed hard and hot against her thigh even through their jeans. "Shay, Shay. I want you."

He brushed her breast and pushed it upward slightly, then buried his face against the soft mound covered by her sweater. Her nipple was swollen with passion under the cotton. His wayward mouth found it and worried it with a flicking tongue. His teeth scraped it gently and nibbled lightly. Sweater and all, he enfolded it in his mouth and tugged rhythmically. Matching that beat, his hips ground against hers.

"Yes, Ian. Please," she called in sporadic pants. "Ian, please."

Then, just as suddenly and as silently as it had begun, the embrace ended. He bolted up from the floor, crossed his arms on the mantel, and rested his forehead against them.

Like a sprung mechanism, she sat upright, too, her body forming a perfect right angle. Rage crept up her shoulders and neck like a tide to flood her face with angry color.

"You . . . you jerk!" she screamed. "Get out. This is the last time you're going to do this to me."

He spun around, towering over her. "Shay, listen. You—"

"*You* listen. I'm a woman. And I love being human flesh and blood. It beats being a cold-blooded bastard like you."

"I know all too well that you're a woman. I—"

"If making love to me is so loathsome, if I'm not wholesome enough, not good enough—"

He dropped down and gripped her shoulders hard, drawing her up and shaking her ruthlessly. His face was fierce in the firelight, with stark planes and ominous shadows. "Don't say—"

"I'll say anything I like."

"Shay, listen to me."

"No! I've had enough of—"

"I love you, damn it," he roared.

His sudden ferociousness, his curse, not to mention what he'd said, stopped her tirade with reverberating abruptness. When she remained speechless, he said more calmly, "Marry me."

Chapter Eight

*I*f he had just confessed to being a drug addict, a
closet pervert, or an axe murderer, she couldn't
have been more dumbfounded. Her mouth went
slack with disbelief. In his eyes she could see
her own reflection, her wide eyes and shocked expression.

When the full impact of his words penetrated, the
tears that had been threatening all day finally came.
She bowed her head and began to sob.

"Shay, what— Why are you crying?"

She flung off his arms, and disregarding the warning he had issued weeks ago, she both cursed him and
pounded his chest with knotted fists. "Damn you!
Damn you! You're cruel. Do you hear me, Reverend
Douglas? Cruel!"

Tears rolled unceasingly down her face as she continued to pummel him. He accepted the blows, making no effort to stop her. At last she slumped against
him exhausted.

"I swear I didn't say that as a way to have sex with you." He framed her face with his hands and tilted it up to look into her swimming eyes. "If that were all I wanted"—he smiled crookedly—"it wouldn't have taken me this long to say a few romantic words."

She gulped, swallowing hard. "Why did you say you loved me? Why did you ask me to marry you?"

"Because I do love you. And I want more than anything for you to be my wife."

She sobbed again, pushing away from him and rising to her feet. "That's impossible! You know it is. Why are you doing this to me?"

He followed her up and grasped her shoulders from behind. "Shay," he said quietly, "do you love me?"

She stopped sobbing, though tears still fell silently down her cheeks. She turned to him and met his inquiring eyes solemnly. "Yes." Her lips trembled, and her hands were shaky as she raised them to his shoulders. She rested her wet cheek against his heart. "Yes, yes, yes." She celebrated the words, chanting them. "It's crazy, ridiculous, but I do love you. I've known I was falling in love with you for weeks, but I didn't want to be." She looked sadly back up at him. "It's hopeless, Ian. Impossible."

He pressed her head back down to his chest and hugged her tightly. His lips moved in her hair. "It's not. We won't let it be impossible."

"But you're you and I'm me and—"

"We complement each other beautifully."

"I can't be a pastor's wife."

"How do you know? You've never tried it. You said yourself that you enjoyed this weekend."

"But a weekend isn't a lifetime."

"And it would be for life, Shay."

"Yes. You'd be stuck with me that long. I'm impetuous, impulsive, irreverent, flamboyant. I have only one dress I can wear to church services, and I wore that today."

He laughed then, rocking her back and forth. "When a woman starts worrying about what she's going to wear, she's as good as convinced."

He stepped back and looked down at her. "Shay, I was happy in my work, but there was no joy in my life. Do you understand? I was becoming staid, placid. You were like an earthquake that shook everything up, turned everything upside down. You gave me an energy I didn't even know I was lacking. I had even come to resent my responsibilities, my church, because they dominated my life so completely. I was busy, but there was no one to share the quiet hours with. You won't be a detriment to my work. You'll add a new dimension to it. You'll balance my world. You're already in my heart, Shay, but I need you in my life, in my bed."

He kissed her gently. She felt powerless to fight him. She was even more ineffectual against the dictates of her own heart. Married life with him would be thoroughly unexpected, but it would be life. Without him, she'd merely go on existing in the wasteland her world had become.

But for their clothes, they would have been making love only moments ago. As her body had arched up to receive the thrusts of his, she had known that she was seeking more than sexual fulfillment. Her heart needed the balm of his love. With him she felt whole, not someone in costume playing out an assigned part.

Being married to him wouldn't be without risks, disappointments, and heartaches. But what marriage was? Perhaps she and Ian had more working against them than for them, but they were both forceful people who didn't back down from challenges.

And they loved each other. Surely that love was worth a few sacrifices.

Her lips opened under his sweet insistence. Once again his hands lifted her sweater and smothered her breasts, which were full and throbbing with love. He lifted his mouth from hers only long enough to say, "Will you marry me, Shay? I'll give you thirty seconds to make up your mind."

Actually he allotted her three days. It was a game. They both knew what her answer would be.

"Shay, if you don't marry me," he said into the telephone late at night on the third day, "you're going to cause me to commit a grievous sin that could curse me to perdition. Do you want that on your conscience?"

"Put that way, you leave me with no choice. Yes, I'll marry you."

He shouted and whooped into the phone for a full five minutes before he settled down to make wedding plans. He didn't want to waste any time, but conceded her two weeks.

The next day she told Vandiveer she was resigning. He took the news as she knew he would—badly.

"Why? Someone else offer to pay you a higher commission? Did you get a permanent modeling job?" His pointed face was pinched with jealous anger.

"No," she said calmly, "I'm taking on the permanent job of being a wife."

"A . . . a wife! To whom?"

"To the man I told you about a few weeks ago."

"The minister!" Shay cringed at his hoot of laughter. "Oh, that's rich. That's the best laugh I've had in months." He eyed her snidely, taking in her mid-calf-length skirt, maroon suede boots, long sweater, and cord belt that was slung low on her hips. "Forgive me for pointing out, my dear, that you're not quite the minister's wife type."

His comment didn't faze her. Grinning broadly, she

placed her hands on her hips, tossed back her mane of wheat-colored hair, and said, "The hell I'm not."

"I can't tell you how happy John and I are," Celia cooed as she helped Shay into her gold satin slip with lace cups that molded her breasts.

Their wedding day had dawned crisp, sunny, and cold. John and Ian's bishop had retired to the living room after the prewedding lunch Mrs. Higgins had provided. Ian had gone into his bedroom to change for the ceremony. Shay had been given one of the spare bedrooms of the parsonage in which to dress.

Shay stilled her mother's busy hands and asked her earnestly, "Are you really happy about it, Mom? Do you think we're doing the right thing? Your endorsement, and John's, mean so much to both of us."

"Of course, we're thrilled about this marriage, Shay dear," Celia exclaimed. "I'll admit to being shocked by your behavior at the cabin that weekend last summer, but then, when hasn't your behavior shocked me? John and I had no idea you and Ian had even seen each other again until you called and told us you were going to spend the weekend here in Brookside. The next thing we knew you were getting married."

"We're so different." Shay voiced aloud the worries she had pondered silently for the last two weeks. Was she making a mistake? Would she be hurt again as she had been by Anson? Worse still, would she hurt Ian in some way?

"I wouldn't let that bother me," Celia said absently, whisking an imaginary piece of lint from Shay's wedding dress. "Those little personality differences add spice to a marriage. Your dress is really lovely, dear."

Shay could argue that their differences weren't exclusively those of personality, nor were they "little." But her mother had diverted her attention to the dress she had selected. It was made of champagne-colored silk and had a slightly blouson bodice. The long sleeves sloped down from the boat neckline and were narrow to her wrists. The skirt was slender with a tulip hem just below her knees. Her mother had loaned her a string of pearls and matching earrings to wear with it. Shay had already pulled her hair into a softly curled topknot.

She was sitting at an old-fashioned vanity table, applying the last touches to her makeup when her mother said, "John has been worried about Ian for years. A man in his position shouldn't be without a wife. He carries a tremendous responsibility, and it isn't healthy for a young man like him not to have an outlet for . . . well, you know," her mother finished, flustered and blushing.

Shay grinned wickedly. "Yes, I know."

"He's been alone for far too long. John said he didn't think Ian would ever get over losing Mary after she was so tragically killed." A sudden pain shafted through Shay, and she set aside her eye crayon and stared blankly at her image in the mirror. "Mary must have been a very special person," Celia went on. "John said she was a precious girl. He said Ian adored her and nearly went mad when she died. She was—"

"Mother," Shay interrupted quickly, "will you excuse me for a minute? I'd like some time to myself."

Celia's chatter broke off, and she looked at Shay, perplexed. "But I wanted to help you dress," she said, hurt showing in her eyes.

"Oh, yes, certainly. I couldn't dress without you. I'll call you when I'm ready. I just need a few minutes alone. You understand. Please?"

"All right," Celia said, going to the door. "I'll be downstairs with Bishop Collins and John. Call when you need me." The door closed softly behind her.

Mary. Mary. Shay had all but forgotten Ian's late wife. Now the memory of their conversation came flooding back. He'd been angry, said he hadn't been intimate with any woman but his wife, said he'd loved her, hadn't remarried . . .

She jumped to her feet and, regardless of her skimpy, sheer attire, walked in stockinged feet down the hall to the door of Ian's room and knocked softly.

"Come on in, Dad," he called.

He was standing at a bureau with his knees bent in order to see into the mirror, brushing his hair. A tight pair of briefs were his only garment. His skin was glowing moistly from his recent shower. The hair dusting his legs and matting his chest was damp and curly. When Shay walked in, he dropped his hairbrush on the dressing table and rushed across the room, his face turning pale at her expression.

"What's the matter, Shay?"

"I have to talk to you."

He pulled her inside and closed the door. Placing his hands on her shoulders, he turned her to face him. "About what?"

"Mary." She could tell by the sudden jumping motion of his dark brows that she'd surprised him. He swallowed hard. Her heart twisted painfully.

"What about her?"

"Everything. I want to know what she was like. How much you . . . how much you loved her. Everything."

"Shay," he said solicitously and raked the line of her jaw with his knuckles, "Mary has nothing to do with us."

"I want to know," she said with a trace of hysteria in her voice. "Now."

He looked intently into her dark eyes. "She was a sweet, lovely woman. Delicate, petite, soft-spoken. She played the piano."

Shay's heart sank to the bottom of her soul like a

lead ball. Mary Douglas had been everything she wasn't, the perfect wife for a dedicated clergyman.

"How long were you married?" she whispered.

"Four years before she was killed." She nodded automatically, dazed. Ian shook her shoulders, and his fingers bit into her tender flesh. "Shay." When she didn't respond, he repeated her name more sharply until she focused her eyes on him. "I loved my wife. I grieved when I lost her. I missed her, but now I love you. Mary is my past and I remember it fondly, but it's over and will never come back. You're my present and my future."

She clutched his naked biceps with frantic hands. "Don't you see, Ian, that we can't go through with this. It's a mistake. I'm nothing like her."

"Absolutely. You're nothing like Mary." She felt the impact of his words like a stabbing dagger, but he went on before she could pull away. "She had none of your marvelous unpredictability. Her emotions weren't erratic and exciting to watch as yours are. She was serene and never expressed herself with fierce passion the way you do."

He closed his arms around her and drew her against the steely length of his body. His breath fanned her neck as he whispered urgently, "Yes, I loved her, Shay. But she was like a milky, polished opal whereas you're a mysterious topaz full of fire, with a thousand dazzling facets. I want us to spend the rest of our lives discovering each one."

He smothered her glad cry with lips that were hot and eager for hers. His tongue probed deeply as though he wanted to touch her soul to convince her of his consummate love.

"I love you, Shay, love you. With all that I am," he said as he tantalized her mouth with airy kisses and flicks of his capricious tongue.

"Ian, I love you so much that I get afraid."

"Never doubt that you aren't everything I want in a wife and in a woman."

The hands closing over her satin-covered derrière were testimony to that. Her arms locked behind his waist as he pressed her against the rigid proof of his love. Like malleable clay, her body conformed to it and harbored it between her thighs. Their heavy sighs of longing harmonized above them only a thudding heartbeat before someone knocked on the door.

"Ian," Bishop Collins said, coming through the door, "you'd better hurry or your bride—" He fell silent when he saw them.

For the first time Shay consciously noted her near nakedness, and she and Ian sprang apart. Ian seemed excruciatingly aware of the evidence of his arousal. Shay splayed her hands over her breasts and whirled around to give the bishop her back, modest and embarrassed for almost the first time in her life.

Bishop Collins harrumphed, and his white brows dropped chastisingly above eyes that danced with wicked delight. "I think the sooner we get to the church the better," he said dryly.

The lights marking the pathways of Central Park twinkled. From the window of their suite at the Plaza Hotel, Shay could see the horse-drawn hansoms lined up, waiting for customers to tour the park. She and Ian would be the residents of the opulent suite for three days, a wedding gift from John and Celia.

She was unaccountably nervous as she stood at the window, knotting, loosening, and reknotting the ribbon tie that held her negligee closed under her bosom.

The wedding ceremony had been the most beautiful experience of her life. In the church amber votives had flickered among greenery and autumn chrysanthemums. While Celia had sniffed daintily from the front pew, Bishop Collins had conducted the ceremony, much of which Shay and Ian had written themselves. It had nothing to do with tradition, with the laws of the state, with anything except the love they were pledging to each other.

Breaking standard practice, Ian led their wedding prayer, invoking God's blessings on their life together. Tears shimmered in Shay's eyes when she lifted her lips for his kiss. Sweet and tender, it conveyed all the love he had for her. It seared her soul and welded it to

Ian's, forming a bond that she knew could never be broken.

Now, waiting for him to come out of the bathroom, she was a bundle of nerves, trembling like the few remaining leaves on the trees in the park that threatened to break away with the next puff of chill air. She didn't know how to act or what to do.

They had embraced numerous times since the night he had proposed. Such embraces had always been ardent. The morning last summer when she had awakened in his arms, his hands and lips caressing her, she had been given a preview of what Ian's lovemaking would be like. He would be earnest and tender, but controlled in his response.

She longed for an adventurous sex life. Only after she'd divorced Anson had she come to realize with maturity that their lovelife had been rather routine. But she didn't expect Ian to share her desire for variety and experimentation.

After all, Mary had died over two years ago. He hadn't been with a woman since then. And he *was* a minister. Wouldn't the normal restrictions that were placed on a man of the cloth in everyday life apply to the marriage bed as well?

If he were awkward or restrained, she'd just have to be patient with him and try not to show her disappointment. She didn't want to shock or offend him on their wedding night. Their sex life may take time to develop to their mutual satisfaction.

The bathroom door opened. The light remained on. Shay shaped her mouth into a smile and turned around. Across the moonlit room, Ian was walking toward her . . . naked.

The shape and symmetry of his limbs was a study in human perfection. He was exactly what she thought God must have had in mind on the day of Creation. The tapering torso with its blanket of dark hair could be envied by even the most virile of men. His sex was bold, proud, unashamed.

Unlike the first time she'd seen him this way, Shay's mouth went dry, and she stammered the first thought that came into her mind. "You . . . you left the light on."

He smiled lazily as he came to her and gently closed his hands around her throat. His thumbs took turns stroking her lips. "I wanted to see you."

"Oh," she replied, nervously twisting her hands between their bodies in the space that was gradually decreasing. "Aren't you cold?"

"How can a man on fire be cold?"

Done with silly conversation, he ducked his head. His tongue outlined her lips leisurely, leaving them dewy and glistening. He almost sipped them dry before he molded his lips to hers, parted them with his tongue, and entered her mouth to taste all of her. His tongue left nothing untouched, exploring with thorough boldness and total possession.

Her knees buckled beneath her, and she clung to him for support. He blazed a hot path of impassioned kisses down the side of her neck to the hollow above her collarbone. "You have on too many clothes," he complained gently.

"Do I?" she breathed, her vision fogged, her ears ringing.

"Uh-huh. May I?" He took her soft moan to be consent and untied the ribbon beneath her breasts. The robe fell away, and he slipped it off her shoulders to float to their feet in a frothy heap.

He murmured his appreciation of the nightgown she had so carefully selected. Lace sheathed the perfect globes of her breasts, her nipples dusky shadows beneath it. The gown fell straight and, clinging, outlined her slender thighs.

"So lovely." He smiled. His hands came up to lightly glide over her breasts. He watched them lovingly as he caressed her, and his eyes became smoky with desire when she felt them blossoming with passion. No longer the shy shadows, her nipples impudently expressed their need. "I want to kiss you here." He took one tightened bud between his fingers and caressed it with almost imperceptible movement.

Her hands fastened on his waist as she swayed toward him and whimpered softly. "Yes, Ian, yes."

He didn't remove the gown immediately, but kissed her through the lace, scratching his limber tongue over the sensitized nipples until Shay's fingers dug into his skin.

"You're sweet, so sweet," he said, finally peeling down the straps of the nightgown. She helped him by shrugging out of it as it settled around her waist. He looked at her breasts and love poured out of his eyes like liquid sapphires. He cradled one lush breast in his palm and lifted it to his thirsting mouth.

He drank his fill while she writhed against him with mounting desire that threatened to destroy her. First one breast, then the other, knew the complete loving of his mouth. He took her nipple and part of the soft mound into that hot, wet mouth and treated it to a gentle suckling before his tongue nudged her nipple to firmer distension.

"Oh, Ian, that feels so good." Her phrases were disjointed from uneven breathing.

"You're delicious." His hand trailed down her spine to the small of her back. When it entangled with the nightgown that still rested there, he brought it down as he followed the womanly curve of her hip.

When she stood as naked as he, he straightened to his full height, took several deep breaths, and said, "I want to look at you. It seems as if I've waited all my life for the privilege."

He took a step backward. His eyes started at the top

of her head. As though seeing her for the first time, he analyzed her irregular halo of golden hair and each feature of her face with adoring, worshipful eyes.

As he continued his visual tour downward, each separate part of her flamed to life: her sloping shoulders and slender throat; her full, round breasts crowned with coral nipples that strained toward him; her narrow waist and flaring hips; her long, pale legs.

He looked up at her and smiled. "Do you remember when you arched your back and thrust your breasts forward that first night while I was drying dishes?"

"You almost dropped the plate."

"I almost dropped my scruples, too. I wanted to rip off your blouse and see if your breasts were as perfect as they promised to be."

"Are you disappointed?"

In answer, he leaned forward and kissed both delicate crests. "Far from disappointed." He cleared his throat and straightened again. "I'm digressing. Turn around."

Docilely she obeyed. He lifted her arms to extend horizontally out from her body. His fingertips traveled down her sides, following the dip of her waist and the curve of her hips. He tested the round fullness of her bottom with gently squeezing hands. On the way back up his hands slid around her body and trailed up her rib cage to close over her breasts. He came up behind her, solid and hard and warm.

With the tip of his nose, he moved her hair aside and whispered in her ear. "You're exquisite."

Her hands folded around his where they held her breasts like cherished works of art. "So are you. I love the way you look. I have from the moment I saw you stepping out of that shower." She twisted, and their mouths met and held for a long kiss over her shoulder.

Without breaking their kiss, Ian turned her to face him and drew her against him in a way that left his level of arousal no secret. Like a rod of velvet-covered steel, his manhood burrowed into her abdomen. "It's time, Shay. I'm going to love you."

He bent slightly at the knees and folded his arms beneath her hips. When he straightened, his head was even with her breasts. He moved his face between them as he carried her to the bed and laid her down. A hospitable housekeeper had turned down the bed while they were at dinner.

She felt like a statue infused with life as she lay there, her hair spread out behind her head on the snowy, scented linen. Her breasts flattened but only slightly when she lay on her back, so well were they fashioned. Her stomach formed a shallow valley beneath her delicate ribcage. A soft, golden tuft of hair at the top of her thighs was a visible reminder that she wasn't marble, but flesh and blood. Shyly alluring, her legs lay together gracefully.

Ian's knees sank into the mattress as he knelt over

her. "I could almost be content just looking at you." He kissed her, his tongue meandering roguishly inside her mouth. "Almost."

His hands fondled her breasts again, his fingertips preparing the way for the lips that closed around nipples aching with love.

Shay wound his glossy black hair around her fingers and held his head fast as it moved with seductive slowness over her body. The daring of his tongue was never ending. On the curves of her breast, the pouting nipples, the dimple of her navel, it danced to an erotic tune. The sweet nibbling of his teeth brought every cell in her body to full awareness. As he dropped rapid, damp kisses on the fevered skin of her abdomen, her muscles contracted in ecstatic reaction.

His inquisitive hands were never satisfied. Repeatedly he caressed her most intimately, whispering how pretty she was there. Her throat arched as her head dug into the pillow. She became mindless to anything but his talented touches and the verbal tributes he paid her.

Her body softened as she allowed his hands and mouth to do as they wished, to shape as they would. She throbbed with a desire so intense that a gasp tore through her lips when his fingers gently parted and tenderly probed the innermost source of her passion.

With softly spoken directions and instructive hands, he positioned them so they might fully enjoy each

Sandra Brown

other. Taking her hand, his tongue rasped across each of her fingertips before he lowered her hand and covered himself with it. "Touch me, Shay." His voice was husky with driving desire, but kind, unhurried, considerate. When she applied a squeezing pressure, she was gratified to hear his ragged sigh of intense pleasure.

She savored the feel of him, his clean scent, the salty taste of his skin. It became of essential importance that she return the love he was giving to her. Her caresses grew bolder, her displays of love unrestricted.

Her eyes fluttered closed, and she trembled in the throes of the fullest stimulation she had ever experienced. His touch was magic. With fingertips, lips, and tongue he caressed parts of her that she now realized had been untouched before. She hadn't known what sexual loving was until this moment of unselfish physical sharing with Ian.

She felt her stomach tighten, and reflexively her thighs did the same. Her breasts quivered with new excitement, and she felt herself slipping off the edge of the world.

But she didn't want to go alone.

"Ian," she called, desperately hoping she had managed to voice that beloved name aloud, for she was moving ever faster toward that splendid oblivion. She pulled unmercifully on his hair until he turned, lifted himself over her, and entered her body.

"Shay. My wife. I love you dearly."

He sank deeper into her tight warmth, and she surrounded him with her love.

When she did fall off the edge of the universe, he was with her, there to catch her to him gently when she coasted back to earth.

"Shay?"

Her whispered name came to her like a ghost. She had awakened with a smile of self-derision on her face. Whatever had made her think Ian might not be an expert lover? He had spent the night proving the contrary to her. Her body was pleasantly replete in the aftermath of his extraordinary lovemaking. Apparently he didn't think the night was over.

"Hmmm?" she mumbled sleepily. She lay on her stomach, her face nestled in the pillow. He was stretched out alongside her, his body partially covering hers. The feel of his resilient body hair on her naked flesh was causing tiny aftershocks of delight, which she'd thought long spent, to erupt again.

"Lift up a little," he urged, as his lips sampled the skin on the back of her neck.

She obliged, and his hands slid beneath her to knead her breasts. He evenly distributed his weight over her as he settled himself between her thighs.

"Oh . . . Ian, that's . . . nice," she said brokenly as his hands once again stirred her to dizzying heights. One smoothed down her stomach to a target eagerly waiting for his touch.

Again he became her teacher, instructing her on how both of them could derive the most pleasure. Before she once again lost her reason, she spoke what was on her mind. "It's never been this way for me, Ian. I . . . ah, darling, that's wonderful . . . I didn't think it would be this way with you."

"How did you think it would be? Not so fast . . . that's it. Perfect, perfect, Shay."

She squeezed her eyes shut and took in a great breath. What he was doing was so sublime, she didn't know if she could speak. "More conventional. We . . ." No, she couldn't mention anyone else's name, not now. It would be profane. And she didn't want to think about Ian and Mary, or her jealousy would kill her. "I knew it could be like this but only through literature, books . . . movies . . ." She broke off with a sigh that spiraled to a musical refrain.

He pressed his face into her spine and rocked upon her slowly. "Never for me either, my love. Never."

Her heart burst with joy. She was unique to him, too. Then, and for a long while later, they found conversation unnecessary.

Chapter Nine

For the next few weeks they were blissfully happy. Shay moved into the parsonage with less awkwardness than she had anticipated. Only one month had remained on the current lease for her apartment. Since the landlord rented it as soon as she gave him notice, the matter was settled with dispatch.

Mrs. Higgins showed pangs of anxiety until Ian assured her that she would continue in her present position. He even suggested she give his bride a few cooking lessons, for which he received a swat on the behind.

Shay undertook the task of redecorating and updating the parsonage. "Nothing much," she said quickly when she saw Ian's wary expression. "Just a few touches here and there. Now that you have a hostess, you should entertain more."

She attacked their bedroom first. Behind the king-sized bed, which Ian had told her had been a Christmas present to himself several years before, she covered the wall with fabric. She spread a quilt in a contrasting color on the bed and heaped it with accenting pillows.

Ian's brows wrinkled as he surveyed her handiwork. "If I'm not tired by the time I go to bed, I'll be exhausted by the time I haul all those pillows off," he said dryly, but she could tell he was pleased.

The changes she made in the living room won even the approval of the Tuesday Morning Bible Study Group. In lieu of one of their meetings, they sponsored a bridal shower for their pastor and his bride. Shay had used her own money to redecorate, not the church's, and the women ooohed and aaahed over the results. Their wedding gifts were generous, and Shay basked in the warmth of their acceptance. Ian smiled proudly and kissed her, to the delight of the ladies, as they were waving them off.

The church building didn't escape Shay's attention either. "Something really should be done in those children's Sunday School rooms," she said one night over dinner.

"Oh, no." Ian groaned. "Here it comes." He took a sip of coffee as if it were an anesthetizing drug. "Okay, let me have it."

Undaunted by his teasing, she said, "They're positively dreary. How can the children learn to appreciate the glory of God when they're surrounded by pea green? The rooms should be bright and cheerful. They should have a bulletin board, pictures on the wall, bean-bag chairs, learning aids—"

"Shay," he said, laying a restraining hand on her arm, "don't you think I'm aware of that? The people who work with the children also know that. But those things cost money. It's not in the church budget this year."

"Money? Is that all?" she said blithely. "Then leave that to me. I'll get the money."

"Shay," he said threateningly, scowling, "what are you up to? You wouldn't do anything that would embarrass me, would you?"

"Isn't this pie delicious? I really should get Mrs. Higgins to teach me how to bake it."

"Shaaaaay," Ian said menacingly.

"What would you say if I told you I didn't. have on any underwear?"

"I'd say you're a shameless disgrace and trying to get me off the subject."

She jumped up from her chair and sailed out the room. "And what would you say if I told you that I'll be naked by the time I reach the bed?"

The Sunday School rooms looked brand-new within two weeks, and the whole congregation was buzzing about it. Shay had invited to dinner a retired paper-mill owner, a member of the church known for his prosperity as well as his stinginess. Ignoring Ian's glowering disapproval, she casually expressed her concern over the dismal rooms. By the time the guest left the parsonage, she not only had his sizable check but also his humble request to assist in the children's departments if that would be all right. Now every Sunday morning he could be found surrounded by enthusiastic children.

"I'd accuse you of manipulation, but the man seems so much happier," Ian said, shaking his head in amazement.

"He was lonely, that's all. He needed to be needed."

When Thanksgiving came around, Shay suggested to the ladies' group that they collect baskets of food for indigent families.

"But there aren't any poor families in our community," one of them protested.

With a vengeance, Shay searched until she found several families in a neighboring town whose main breadwinner had been laid off from his or her job. None of the families were members of the church, but by Thanksgiving week the bed of a pickup truck was filled to the brim with staples. A grocer had donated three dressed turkeys, and businessmen in the congregation were looking for positions in their companies for the people who were unemployed.

Feigning jealousy, Ian complained. "When the telephone rings, it's for you now instead of me." It was

Saturday morning. Since Mrs. Higgins was off, Shay had cooked him a late brunch.

"Nonsense," she said, plopping down in his lap, wrapping her arms around his neck, and settling her mouth over his.

They both sighed resignedly when the telephone rang. Shay stretched to reach for the receiver.

"Hello . . . Oh, yes, Mrs. Turner," she said, sticking her tongue out at Ian's "I-told-you-so" look. "Mrs. Graham had her baby last night? A boy? How wonderful! I'll be sure to tell Ian so he can go see her at the hospital this morning. You're right." Shay began unsnapping her quilted robe until her body, warm and rosy beneath, was fully revealed to Ian. "We should take meals to her family while she's in the hospital. When she gets out, I think we should schedule volunteers to go over each afternoon to help with dinner, don't you?" Without the least change of inflection in her face, she took his hand and placed it over her breast. "Maybe for that first week . . . Thank you. I can't think of anyone better to organize it . . . Okay, I'll tell him . . . Good-bye."

Shay's invitation was more than Ian could resist. Leaning forward, he nuzzled her with his nose and mouth, fondling her with a touch that never failed to arouse her.

"Tell me what?" he mumbled against the velvet cleft between her breasts.

Throwing her head back wantonly, she sighed as his tongue rolled over her tautening nipple. "Tell you that Mrs. Graham is resting, and her doctor requested no visitors until later today."

"Remind me to thank that doctor the next time I see him," he said, sweeping her into his arms and heading for the stairs.

The first blowup came two weeks later, just before Christmas. They had spent a quiet evening decorating the tall tree in the living room, sipping hot cider, and enjoying the fireplace and each other's company. Their love play and frequent kisses had stirred them to desire. They were on their way upstairs when the doorbell pealed.

It was a man from church asking quietly to speak to Ian in private. Ian showed the man into his study, then returned to Shay. "Warm up my spot," he said, patting her fanny lightly and kissing her quickly.

Upstairs, she took a long bubble bath, smoothed a rich lotion all over her body, buffed her nails, and climbed into the wide bed to wait for her husband.

Impatient after an hour had dragged by while she tried to read a less-than-engrossing book, she pulled on a modest robe and went downstairs.

By now Shay was accustomed to members of Ian's congregation calling him at home or cornering him for conversation when they were out in public. Often they bent his ear for no reason other than because they were lonely and needed a sounding board. He always listened patiently, even when they became long-winded. But their visitor tonight was the most verbose of all! No doubt Ian was looking for a tactful way to conclude the visit.

Shay grinned impishly as she devised a plan to relieve Ian of their uninvited guest and at the same time get her husband up to bed where he belonged. Conveniently there was a pad and pen on the foyer table.

A few minutes later, she tapped lightly on the door of Ian's study. "Yes?" he called.

She went in, not looking at the visitor, only her husband. "I'm sorry to disturb you, but someone called and left this emergency message for you."

Ian, his face expressionless, looked at her, then at the telephone, which hadn't rung for hours, then back up at her. He took the piece of folded paper she extended to him, unfolded it, and read the message: *"Your place in the bed is warm, and there's a hot woman waiting for you. Send him home! Signed, The Hot Woman."*

The secret smile curving her mouth collapsed when she saw Ian's furious expression. "Thank you," he said tersely, barely moving his lips.

"You're welcome," she said haughtily. Her shoulders back and chin up, she stalked proudly out of the study and up the stairs. Reaching their room, she whipped off her robe and the sexy negligee it had concealed and pulled on a long, flannel nightgown.

Too enraged to cry, she fumed, pounding her pillow and thumping the covers when they wouldn't cooperate with her thrashing limbs. Since she couldn't sleep, she tried to read again. The words blurred before her eyes, she was so angry for his ignoring her.

But when she heard his footsteps on the stairs, her heart lurched with fear. She had seen hints of Ian's temper before and had dreaded the first time she'd experience its full impact. She knew that time had come the instant the door was flung open and just as quickly slammed shut behind him.

"Don't ever do anything like that again." His eyes flashed with anger. "*Never* again. Do you understand?"

She flew off the bed, sending pillows scuttling and her unread book sliding to the floor. "No, I don't understand."

"Then let me explain it to you. That man's world is crumbling around him. He needed help, counsel. Thank God he came to me for whatever assistance I might provide instead of seeking solace in a bottle or blowing his brains out, both of which he confessed had occurred to him.

"Then, right in the middle of a counseling session that was crucial to this man's peace of mind, if not his life, you come in flaunting a ribald note in my face.

How could I talk to him, pray with him, with that kind of distraction?"

Tears filled her eyes. "It wasn't ribald. I'm your wife."

"Then you should know better than to interrupt when I'm counseling someone in need."

"And what about me? What if I need you too?"

"You'll have to learn to wait."

"But I'm your *wife*," she repeated. "I come first."

He stared at her for a long moment, then said in a low voice that reverberated through the room, "No, Shay, God comes first."

Her face drained of all color, and she felt her life was seeping out of her body. Blindly she turned and fled to the bathroom, shutting and locking the door behind her. Only then did she let the tears fall. They flowed down her cheeks in torrents while wracking sobs shook her body.

"Shay, open this door," Ian demanded, knocking on it from the other side. "I'm sorry I yelled at you. Now open the door."

She obeyed him, opening the door immediately, flinging herself repentantly into his arms, and hugging him tight.

"I'm sorry, I'm sorry," she said. "I didn't know. Honestly I didn't. I'm a wretched wife."

He buried his face in her wealth of hair and drew

her toward the bed. There he comforted her until her crying had stopped and she was hiccuping softly.

"You didn't know any better this time. Ordinarily I would love to get a naughty note from you. It wasn't the note I objected to. It was your timing. I try to schedule counseling sessions during the day at my church office when I know I won't be disturbed. This was an emergency, and the first one since our marriage. I should have prepared you for nights like this, times when the telephone will ring and I'll have to leave you and our bed with virtually no explanation."

"I know, I know. Mentally I know that God and your work have to come first in your life. Forgive me for my occasional lapses of jealousy," she said, moving her fingers over his face, loving him. "It wasn't malicious. I didn't realize the gravity of his coming. I thought he had just come to visit. I'm trying, Ian. I really am."

He hugged her harder, running his hands over her back. "I know you are, and I'm so proud of you it's almost sinful."

She laughed then and pushed away, looking at him with her eyes awash with tears. "I love you so much."

"I love you, too," he whispered and lowered his mouth to hers for a kiss that drew her soul into his. "I love you." He covered her face and throat with kisses that grew in urgency even as his hands became greedier in their caresses. "What are you doing in this shroud?" he asked, pulling at yards of flannel in an effort to touch her. Hastily they undressed, and he pulled her down on top of him on the bed. "I do love you, Shay."

"I know, I know. I'm ashamed and sorry for what I did tonight. I was unthinking and selfish."

"I'll give you an opportunity to be unselfish."

She smiled and, leaning forward, offered him her breasts.

The candlelight service Ian conducted at midnight on Christmas Eve was one of the most moving Shay had ever attended. Christmas Day was a happy occasion, which they spent at the parsonage with Celia and John, who seemed more in love than ever. Members of the church dropped by bearing gifts in appreciation of Ian's devoted service to them through the year. Mrs. Higgins kept coffee, hot cranberry punch, and baked goods in ready supply for such unannounced guests.

Shay suggested that Ian open one of his presents from her in private. It was a box of body paints that they tried out in the shower while Celia and John retired to the guest bedroom for an afternoon nap.

"Isn't this fun?" Shay smoothed a line of Passionate Purple down his chest and stomach. His breath lodged in his throat when her fingers slid farther down.

"It's decadent." Despite his hoarse voice, he was accurately applying a dab of Voluptuous Vermilion to her nipple. "I think this is what they were doing in Sodom and Gomorrah before the Lord destroyed it."

"What a way to go," she said against his mouth.

They dropped tubes of paint onto the shower floor as their searching hands found better occupations. She swayed against him hypnotically, her thighs grazing elusively over his lower body until he trembled with need. "Shay, I can't wait. Take me inside you."

He grasped her hips with strong hands, and she let herself be impaled on his strength. Her cries of ecstasy echoed in the small tile enclosure as he fused their bodies with the wet, sleek precision of two sea creatures. Their mating was frenzied and quick. His body shuddered with his release at the same moment that she collapsed onto his chest, dying a little even as his life pumped into her.

Afterward they clung together weakly as water sluiced over them and cooled their fevered bodies. They fell apart, stunned, when they heard someone knocking on the bathroom door.

Ian shut off the water. "Yes?" he croaked.

"I hate to bother you, Ian," Celia called, "but I couldn't find Shay. There's a group of people from the church waiting to see you. I've served them refreshments in the living room."

"Th–thank you," he stuttered, Shay's playful hands giving him no respite. "We'll . . . I'll be right down."

He took her hands away and held them off him. "Let's try to get respectable."

Fifteen minutes later they were the picture of decorum as they descended the stairs, Shay's arm folded in the crook of Ian's elbow.

"I'm sorry we were . . . uh . . . busy when you arrived." Ian addressed the group politely from the wide door of the living room.

"We were doing some painting in the bathroom," Shay said with a deceptively angelic smile. Surreptitiously Ian pinched her on the bottom, and everyone jumped in startled surprise when their minister's wife yelped loudly for no apparent reason. "Won't you have some punch?" she said graciously and much more humbly as her husband led her into the living room.

The new year promised them happiness. Every day Shay came to love her husband more. She had been welcomed into the church with loving arms, and though some people found her way of accomplishing things a bit unorthodox, they couldn't criticize what she accomplished.

Shay found doing projects around the church immensely satisfying, but not quite energy-taxing enough to suit her. When a charming shop on the square attracted her attention, she bought several items for the parsonage there. The stock wasn't as elite as what Vandiveer had carried, but the gift boutique had a certain warmth that appealed to her. She made the acquaintance of the owner, and when she learned that his assistant was taking pregnancy leave in the spring, she applied for the job. It was only for three afternoons a week, but it would fill in the extra time she had on her hands. When she mentioned her plans to Ian, the idea met with his wholehearted approval. Shay was impatient for spring to arrive so she could begin working.

One snowy afternoon, Ian returned home stamping slush off his boots, clapping his gloved hands together, and shouting at the top of his lungs. Shay was stirring a pot of homemade soup at the range. She whirled toward him with excitement, her cheeks flushed.

"Guess what!" they said in unison, then laughed together.

"You go first," she said.

"No, you."

"Mine's better. You go first."

He pulled off his gloves with his teeth and clasped her shoulders with cold, red hands. "The basketball team is going to the tri-state playoffs, and they've asked me to go along." His blue eyes sparkled like a child's. He assumed a solemn expression and cleared his throat pedantically. "For spiritual guidance, of course."

"Oh, darling, that's great."

"I get to ride on the bus and everything."

She laughed at his boyish enthusiasm.

"Now you tell me your news. But first a kiss." He bent to plant a hard, damp kiss on her mouth as his hand stole under her sweater.

"Ach!" she wailed, spinning away from him. "That's cold."

"Come on," he said, stalking her around the kitchen, his arms outstretched, his lips smacking the air in an exaggerated pucker. "Give me a kiss."

She laughed and tossed a dish towel over his head. "Not on your life. Not until you warm up those hands."

"Tell me what's got you so excited," he said, pouring himself a cup of coffee from the pot she had warming on the stove.

"You'll never guess. My agent called, and Peter Zavala wants to photograph me. He's been asked to do a one-man show at the Metropolitan Museum next summer. I'm only one of many models he'll test-photograph, of course," she went on excitedly, "but he wants to do the entire study around one model. If I'm the one selected, I can't tell you what it would do for my career."

"Or mine." His comment echoed in the sudden silence between them.

She stared at him. Her first reaction was a flare of

temper. She'd thought he'd be glad for her. Instead his face looked like a thundercloud as he stared into his coffeecup. In an effort to keep their relationship on an even keel, she licked her lips and said patiently, "He's the best, Ian. He specializes in photographing women. He's right up there with Avedon and Scavullo. It's an honor even to be asked to pose for him."

Ian pushed angrily away from the counter. "I know who he is. I've admired his work. I'm not that much a provincial puritan, as you're so fond of calling me."

"Well, then you can appreciate—"

"I can't appreciate my wife getting excited about taking off her clothes and posing for a photographer, and I don't care if he's the King of Siam!" he shouted. "Furthermore, I can't think of anything worse than having you displayed in the Metropolitan Museum, sprawling naked for all the world to see."

Rage, hot and fierce, coursed through her veins. "I do not *sprawl*," she retorted. "Zavala takes classic photographs, beautiful studies of the human body."

"And we all know how proud you are of your human body, don't we? You're always eager to show it off."

"And you're always damn eager to look!" she shouted. It was the first time she had cursed in weeks, and the word felt strange on her tongue.

"I'm your husband!"

"But not my owner, nor my conscience. Other people may come to you for advice about what they should do, but I don't need to. I know what I want. And what I want right now is to pose for Zavala." With that she left the room.

She didn't come down for dinner. Ian stayed in his study for most of the night. When at last he came to bed, she pretended to be asleep. The rest of the week followed the same pattern. There was no intimacy between them, barely any conversation beyond what was necessary. The tension in the house was palpable.

She didn't see him the morning of her appointment in Manhattan. He'd already left the house when she came downstairs, but she had arranged for Mrs. Higgins to drive her to the train station. She boarded the train with a leaden heart, resenting Ian. He should feel proud that she'd been asked. He should encourage her, calm her nerves, buck up her spirits. This assignment was important to her.

As the miles ticked off under the train's wheels, her bitterness increased and her determination along with it. She wouldn't let him spoil this opportunity for her. When she entered the studio, she'd be wonderful—animated, alive, and glowing.

She was. But when the session finally ended at nine o'clock that evening, she was exhausted. After checking into the most inexpensive hotel she could find in which she'd feel safe, she called home.

"Yes?" Ian said into the telephone. Was there a worried, anxious tone in his voice?

"Ian, it's me. I'm still in New York, and since it's so late, I've decided to spend the night and catch the first train home in the morning."

"I see," he said rigidly. "Do you have enough money, everything you need?"

"Yes."

"Well, then call Mrs. Higgins when you arrive, and she'll pick you up."

"All right." A lump of regret as hard as a rock was lodged in her throat. She wanted to talk to him, to tell him that since he hadn't endorsed it, posing for Zavala hadn't been nearly as exciting as she had expected. He had been demanding, condescending, and petulant.

Now, hearing Ian's voice, she wanted to cry, to tell him how tired she was, how much she hated this animosity between them, how much she missed his tender, ardent lovemaking. But pride wouldn't let her. Damn him! He'd backed her into a corner, and she couldn't relent. "Well, good night then."

"Good night." He hung up without another word.

The next day, Mrs. Higgins met Shay's train and dropped her at the house on her way to the market. "Reverend Douglas is at home," she told Shay as she got out of the car. Not finding him on the lower floor, Shay went upstairs. Her heart constricted with fear when she entered the bedroom and saw Ian tossing clothes into a suitcase. Was he leaving her?

"Ian?"

He turned around. "Hello, Shay. How was your trip?"

"What are you doing?" she asked, disregarding his inquiry. "Where are you going?"

"To the basketball playoffs, remember?"

She released a pent-up breath. "Oh, yes. When?"

"Right now."

Disappointment swamped her. She had hoped they might settle the misunderstanding between them today. "I see. For how long?"

He snapped the suitcase shut and pulled it off the bed. "Until they lose a game." He brushed past her and made his way downstairs. "I've asked Mr. Griffin, who is chairman of the deacons, to oversee things at the church while I'm gone. I'm to be called if there's an emergency. Otherwise refer anyone who calls about church business to him."

"I will," Shay replied, following him despondently down the stairs.

He shrugged into his coat at the door and pulled on his gloves. "The coach's wife will know where we're staying if you need me."

I need you! she cried silently. "Ian." The desperation in her voice must have registered on him. He turned on his way out the door. Snowflakes settled on his dark hair and lashes.

"Yes?"

She wanted to fly into his arms, to mesh her mouth with his, to taste his passion, to take his strength into herself. But angry, hateful words echoed loudly in her head. She wasn't ready to capitulate, and she knew he wouldn't.

She shook her head. "Nothing. Have a safe trip."

"Good-bye."

The door closed solidly behind him, like the door of a cell. Shay felt imprisoned by despair—total, black, and absolute.

Chapter Ten

*S*now continued to fall for hours after Ian left. Shay was forced to stay inside. When the heavy snow didn't stop, and it looked like driving would become difficult, she sent Mrs. Higgins home for the duration of the storm. Shay didn't want to worry about the older woman driving to and from the parsonage in dangerous weather.

Shay roamed the cheerless, empty rooms, listening unconsciously for the sound of Ian's voice, the stamp of his boots, his low husky laughter, his whispered words of love. Those were the dearest to recall, but they brought waves of loneliness.

"I love for you to touch me there," she had said the last time they'd made love.

"Here?"

There had followed a long pause as their rasping breath filled the still room. "Yes."

"I love touching you. Soft, womanly."

His gifted fingers, which contained all the secrets

of loving, prepared the way for a sweet mouth and a nimble tongue. Love flowed through her body like a fine wine, rich and pure, effervescent and intoxicating.

Wrapping her arms around herself now, Shay felt an emptiness yawning wide inside her as she remembered all the times they had made love. Sometimes they had been playful and swift, coming to a lusty completion quickly. Other times they had been slow and languid, drawing out each other's passion for hours until they allowed themselves the pleasure of explosive culmination. But always it had been an exchange, not only of their bodies, but of their spirits as well. Shay missed that most of all.

The basketball tournament dragged on for days. Shay listened to it on the radio, feeling closer to Ian that way. But as Brookside continued to win, Ian remained absent, and a new suspicion began to haunt her. For several days now she had been feeling vague changes in her body. Her period was over a week late—and as a rule she was as regular as clockwork. Alone in the empty house without Ian to share her thoughts, she grew increasingly restless. Finally she decided to brave the still snow-covered streets. She drove to a nearby pharmacy and bought a pregnancy testing kit, which she knew to be fairly reliable.

When she returned home, she sat for hours, staring contemplatively into the fire, her hands folded across her stomach, thinking about much more than just the results of the test she was waiting for.

It came to her quietly then that she knew what Ian's sermon had been about that first morning she'd heard him speak. She knew, too, what she must do.

When they had married, she'd known she loved him, but not until recently had she realized the magnitude of her love and what it required of her. She would give up her modeling, at least the nude modeling. She would give it up freely, not because Ian had demanded it of her, but because she loved him and couldn't live with anything that made him unhappy. At one time such self-denial would have been impossible for her. She would have thought someone expected it of her, and she would have resented Ian for not accepting her as she was. Now her decision didn't feel like self-denial at all. And when she went upstairs to the bathroom and saw that the test results were positive—she was pregnant!—she experienced a fulfillment and peace she'd never known in her life. Oh, if only Ian would hurry home!

Suddenly she was injected with renewed energy. Since her job at the small boutique hadn't started and the weather prohibited everything else, she raided the pantry and spent the afternoon preparing casseroles and baked goods that she could freeze for later. She sang as she worked and laughed aloud when she realized that she was humming the tune Ian had been singing in the shower that first day. How long ago that seemed now. She wasn't the same shallow, flighty girl she'd been then. A woman had emerged in her place, a woman who knew what it meant to be loved. She only wished Ian were here so she could share her new understanding with him.

When the phone rang, she all but lunged for it, hoping, praying it would be Ian so she could tell him all that she had discovered in his absence.

"Mrs. Douglas, this is the fire chief. Is your husband there?"

"I'm sorry, he's out of town. Can I help you?" The man's shouting voice told her he was probably calling from a mobile telephone—which indicated an emergency situation.

"We've got a hell of a fire at the Shady Oaks apartment complex." He didn't seem to notice his slip of the tongue and neither did Shay. "The people who don't require hospitalization need someplace warm to go. Could we use the church until their friends or families can be notified to pick them up?"

"You can use it for as long as anyone needs it. Bring them there immediately. To the basement. I'll meet you to make sure the furnace is on."

"Some of them are in pretty bad shape, Mrs. Douglas. I hate to dump this on you, but—"

"I'll see that they're taken care of. Were there any . . . casualties?"

"I'm afraid so, Mrs. Douglas."

She gripped the receiver and forced down the bile that flooded the back of her throat. "I'm on my way."

She made three calls, delegating responsibility for blankets, food, and first aid, which was to be provided as soon as possible. Then she called Mr. Griffin at his hardware store and told him to go to the church immediately to see that the furnace was started and to do anything else he saw necessary to aid those who would be sheltered there. Then she called the hotel where she knew Ian was staying. Days ago, when she thought she might die of loneliness, Shay had asked the coach's wife where to reach him. She'd asked for the information, but because she was too proud, she hadn't been able to bring herself to call him.

Now when she did, she learned that he wasn't in his room. She left an urgent message. Then, taking up what she thought she might need for an indefinite vigil, she banked the fire in the fireplace, locked the house, and left for the church.

The following hours were a nightmare. Exhausted firemen and policemen led frightened, grief-stricken, disoriented people into the basement. Children cried for parents from whom they'd been separated. Frantic mothers called desperately for children they couldn't find. Old people wandered around dazed, lost, and weeping.

Shay learned that the fire had been caused by an

explosion in a furnace that had ripped through the walls and ceiling of the complex with rampant destruction. Black, oily smoke had filled exit hallways. Ceilings had collapsed, blocking people's escape. Those who had survived were numb with the shock of having lost all their possessions.

Shay worked endlessly through the night, doing what she could to comfort body and soul. For those who had arrived shivering and half-clothed, their garments having been burned or torn away, she provided warm blankets. Other women of the church prepared and served a hearty soup. Drawing upon what she'd learned in a Red Cross course on emergency aid, Shay bandaged those injuries that weren't serious enough to warrant hospital treatment. She massaged life back into fingers and toes that had been exposed to the freezing cold.

Continuing reports from the site of the fire became more grim with each passing hour. The number of casualties rose as firemen finally got the flames under control and began digging through the wreckage. The hospital was reportedly filled to overflowing with burn victims.

Shay issued orders like a general, sang lullabies, and prayed. She seemed to be everywhere at once, answering hundreds of questions, giving assistance to all who required it.

When one of the women became hysterical when

her husband's body was reported found, she called the Catholic priest to come. She was grateful when the rabbi of the local synagogue arrived to comfort those who were asking for him. When Mr. Griffin's brows rose with disapproval, Shay ignored him. Ian would have done the same.

She managed to sleep for a few hours in the early morning before the survivors began to stir. Her back ached with weariness, and her temples throbbed when she rose, but she was smiling gently as she coaxed a three-year-old crying for his mother to eat a scrambled egg. She was holding the child on her lap, pushing a bite of egg through quivering lips, when she saw Ian standing in the doorway.

Their eyes locked across the room, and for a moment her heart seemed to stop. Tears of gladness filled her bleary eyes. He was there. Things would get better.

He wended his way through the cots the National Guard had provided after Shay had demanded them. He squatted down beside her chair. "I'm sorry I wasn't here."

"We've managed, but I'm so glad to see you." Her lips were quivering.

Ian ran a comforting hand over the child's curly head. "Where's his mother?"

A tear rolled down Shay's cheek. She shook her

head. "Both his parents. His grandmother is coming for him when she can get here."

Ian nodded. He took the child's hand and pressed it to his cheek. He closed his eyes tightly. Shay had never loved him more than at that moment. Finally he opened his eyes and stood up. "Many of the roads are still blocked with snow. I rented a car the minute I got your message and drove all night." He touched her cheek almost shyly. "How are you?"

She shook her head to dismiss such a silly question at a time like this. "*They* need you now, Ian." She nodded toward the other people in the crowded room.

He nodded. "I'll see you later."

By the end of the second day, the basement had been cleared of people. Shay could have gone home, but after assigning a crew to restore the basement and return borrowed equipment, she set about gathering up clothing for people who had survived. She visited those in the hospital who were able to have visitors. She tracked down vacancies in other apartment complexes for those who had been left homeless.

Ian buried the dead and comforted their families. He worked tirelessly with a crew clearing out the wreckage, trying to locate personal belongings that might be salvaged. The weather cooperated. It was still bitterly cold, but there was no more snow.

Celia and John called and offered to come and help.

Shay and Ian urged their parents to stay home. They went their separate ways in the mornings and returned late in the evenings to eat the dinner Mrs. Higgins left in the oven and then fell exhausted into bed. They couldn't deal with guests underfoot—even guests willing to help.

Within a week things more or less returned to normal. Shay returned home from the hospital early one afternoon and suddenly realized that nothing required her immediate attention. She laid wood and kindling in the fireplace, prepared a salad to go with the pot roast Mrs. Higgins had cooked that morning, and set the table in the dining room. Those chores done, she went upstairs to shower and change.

She was in the kitchen, watching for Ian's station wagon to pull into the driveway, when the telephone rang. Her agent's voice came as a complete surprise. He had called to tell her that Zavala wanted to use her, but that he wanted to have another session. He was pleased with her, but the pictures he'd taken didn't satisfy him.

Shay took a deep breath. "I hate to do this to you," she said, "but I don't think I'll do this one . . . I know, but— . . . Well, I'm sorry, but I don't think I want to work with him . . . I don't care, he wasn't professional and threw about six temper tantrums while I was there. I don't need that. I was paid for that session only, not for the job itself, so he can't use the pho-

tographs without my permission. Besides, there's another reason, one more important . . . No, it isn't that.
I'm going to have a baby . . . No, I'm thrilled—No, I
don't think so unless it's a really special job . . . Perhaps. I'll have to talk to Ian about it . . . Okay. I'm
sorry about the Zavala thing . . . Thank you . . . Good-
bye."

Pensively she returned the telephone receiver to the
wall hook. There, it was done. And she felt no sense
of loss. With a secret smile on her face she turned—
and saw Ian standing in the doorway. She froze. For
long moments she tried to read his mood and couldn't.
Finally she said lamely, "I didn't hear you come in."

His eyes roved over her face like darts seeking a
target. He still wore his coat, muffler, and gloves. A
puddle of melting snow was forming around his
boots. "You're going to have a baby?" he asked
huskily.

She nodded, feeling a pang of anxiety. Would he be
pleased?

But her worries were unnecessary. He stumbled toward her, dropping his outdoor wear, letting the pieces
fall where they may. He reached out to touch her, hes-
itated, pulled his hand back, and looked down at her
stomach, which was as flat as it had ever been.

She smiled tenderly. "You can touch me. As a matter of fact, I'd be pleased if you would."

"Shay," he said in a way that made the word part

apology, part relief. He drew them to the wall, leaning his shoulder and head against it and laying a sensitive hand on her abdomen. "A baby," he whispered. "Our baby." His hand pressed tenderly. "Shay, I've been so miserable," he admitted.

She turned her face into the collar of his shirt, pressing her nose into that triangle at the base of his throat and breathing deeply of the masculine scent she loved. "I have, too. I've wanted you so much. Missed you, missed the closeness we had."

Keeping one hand pressed to her stomach, he tilted her head up with the other. "It's been so long, I've almost forgotten what it tasted like to kiss you."

She gave him a teasing smile. "Please feel free to revive your memory."

His lips were firm and surprisingly warm considering he'd just come in from outside. They parted gently and hers responded, following suit. For a moment they held there, motionless save for the breath that wafted between them. His fingers moved lovingly down her stomach, cupping the place where his child grew in her body.

She felt him shudder as love swept through him. He uttered a low, gratified moan at the instant his tongue entered her mouth in a gentle violation. A welcome marauder, it probed and stroked, rapidly one moment, slowly the next, in ever-changing tempos that captivated her senses.

"Let's go to bed," he said, when at last he sacrificed the nectar of her mouth for the warm, scented skin of her neck.

"What about dinner?" she queried weakly.

"Later."

He carried her up the stairs, their eyes telegraphing a thousand messages of love. They undressed each other with a titillating leisure, watching each other, devouring each other with hungry eyes. Climbing beneath the covers from opposite sides of the bed, they met in the middle.

"Hold me," Shay pleaded, wrapping her arms around his waist. "Hold me."

Their hearts pulsed together, no longer separate but two parts of a whole. His head sheltered hers beneath his chin. From shoulder to toes they touched.

"I behaved just like the stupid, narrow-minded prude you once accused me of being," he confessed. "Why didn't you sock me in the gut the way you did the first time?"

"Don't think I wasn't tempted," she said, smiling and loving the feel of his chest hair against her lips. "I didn't think it through, Ian, or I never would have suggested I pose for Zavala."

"No, no. You were totally justified in wanting to do the job. I should have shared your excitement. I'm proud of your body. Why shouldn't I be elated at the thought of your beauty being exhibited? I was a jackass. I acted just the way I counsel headstrong, possessive husbands not to act. I've always been a proponent of equality in marriage, but when it came to my own, I didn't practice what I preached."

She snuggled closer. "After I got to the studio, I didn't want the job. Your disapproval had taken the joy out of it."

"See?" he exclaimed in self-flagellation. "That's what I mean. I feel like I've cheated you out of something important."

She raised her head to look at him. "You haven't, Ian. I don't want anything in my life that we can't share. Besides, Zavala was a jerk. He cursed me, his camera, his lights, his assistants. He pouted, paced, smoked about six joints, hit—"

Ian bolted upright, his eyes blazing and nostrils flaring. "Joints! Hit? Hit what?"

"Calm down," she said, ruffling his hair affectionately and enjoying his show of temper because it was in her defense. "Hit the wall with his fist. That kind of nonsense I can live without. I told you before that I was particular." She pulled him back down on the pillow, though she kept her hands entwined in his hair. The black strands coiled around her fingers like silk.

"You're not going to retire completely, are you? From this end it sounded like your agent mentioned another job to you."

"Well, yes," she hedged, not sure how he'd take her news.

"Tell me."

"*Life* magazine is looking for a pregnant lady their cameras can follow through the early stages right up to the day of birth. A medical team will assist with the photography. They want a pictorial document of the pregnancy, growth of the fetus, and the birth."

"You mean my son will be in *Life?*" Ian beamed.

"So it's okay for your son to be photographed in the nude, but not your wife! And who said it was a son?"

He laughed and hugged her to him. "I rather like the idea of both of you being celebrities. I'd like to talk to the people in charge of the project. I don't want you endangered under any circumstances."

"I wouldn't have it any other way. This should be a family project or not at all."

"I'll never be so uncompromising again, Shay. I swear it. You said you couldn't be stifled. I don't intend to try."

"And I'll never act like a headstrong, spoiled brat again either. I want your opinion on everything I do." She laid her cheek on the hair-roughened skin of his chest. "You were right about me, Ian, from the very beginning. I was playing a role. I wanted to appear flippant and uncaring because I was insecure about the person I really am. My father wanted me to be a rebel. He had a devilish bent that loved for me to pull a prank. He actually encouraged my outrageousness. My mother wanted me to be a lady. She always disapproved of my behavior.

"I was trapped somewhere in between, but it was easier to be naughty and please my father than to be nice and please my mother. I never felt like a real person, but two parts constantly warring with each other. It took your love to bring out the real me."

"I love all the facets of you. I've told you that."

"You're generous with your love. As far as working again, I'm not making any plans. The baby may change my figure completely." Idly she feathered her hand back and forth across the curve of his buttocks. "Besides, I'll have plenty to keep me busy around here with you, the baby, my job in the afternoons at the boutique, and the church."

"I think you can count on that, especially after this past week. You've shown a remarkable knack for getting things done." He traced the fragile line of her collarbone with his finger. "Everyone loves you, Shay."

"I'm glad. Not for my sake, but for yours."

"All week I've heard endless praise for how you responded to the emergency. From the fire chief on down, I've heard nothing but compliments." His mouth twitched with amusement as his fingertip traced her mouth. "Except for Mr. Griffin. He saw you kick the stove and swear at it when it wouldn't light right away."

"That tattletale!" she cried indignantly. She buried her face against his chest. "Did I kick the stove and swear? I don't remember."

He chuckled. "He did admit you were in somewhat of a state." His index finger under her chin raised her face back to his. "You may be nominated for canonization before it's all over."

"Do you want me to be a saint?" Her breath fanned his chest as her lips toyed with his nipple. "All the time?"

"In public, maybe. In my bed I rather like you to show a streak of wickedness."

"That won't taint your admiration of me?" She flicked a pink tongue over his skin, proof that her wicked streak was very much still a part of her.

"That's what I had in mind for right now. Admiring you." In one agile motion he swept the covers aside and turned her on her back. His eyes made a swift, ravaging tour before returning to her face to begin again with leisure.

He covered her face with soft, fluttery kisses. "I'll never forget what this face looked like when I first saw it in a bathroom mirror."

"I'll never forget what I first saw either . . . even before your face." She touched him and grinned when he stirred with arousal.

"You're shameless. Imagine taking advantage of a poor, defenseless man that way."

"Yes, just imagine." She was taking even greater liberties now, caressing his hard, virile shape with loving fingers.

"I'm only going to give you forty years to stop doing that," he rasped unsteadily. His tongue batted at her earlobe, then delicately investigated the interior until her back arched and she demanded his kiss.

Their lips flirted, sliding against each other as they moved their heads from side to side. Her tongue teased the corner of his mouth, and his outlined the shape of hers. All of this was only a preamble to their mating when their tongues penetrated each other's mouth, thrusting and withdrawing until they both had to come up for air.

"I'll never be appeased," he vowed. "You only make me hungry for more." Sliding down her body, he examined her breasts with luminous eyes. Experimentally he touched her nipple and watched it stiffen beneath his finger. His tongue licked it lightly. He looked down at it and whispered, "Beautiful," before he took the firm bud between his lips and drew it into his mouth. When both nipples had been treated to that kind of loving, he adored their wet glossiness with avid eyes.

"Let me love you, too," she begged.

"Soon. I told you there was so much of you to admire."

He kissed his way down her stomach. His tongue

dipped into her navel in playful forays until Shay whimpered helplessly. He gave special attention to the gentle mound where their child slept and paid homage to her femininity. He was the most ardent of lovers, kissing her intimately, loving her unselfishly, bringing her to a pinnacle of passion she'd never reached before.

"Please," she sobbed, clutching at him.

His hands slid beneath her back, and he lifted her up and over him as he levered himself on his knees. With their hearts drumming together, he entered her, piercing her heart and breaking it open with his love. It showered them both with sparks of light that would burn into infinity.

She fell against him, gasping for air. He held her tightly until they both quieted, stroking down from the top of her head to the graceful fullness of her hip with a loving hand. Gradually he lowered them both to the bed. He didn't leave her but lay nestled inside as she smiled up at him, drowsing in the aftermath of a tempest.

"Are you sure you've always been a minister?" she asked sleepily, brushing back tousled raven strands from his forehead.

"Why do you ask?" He kissed the sheen of perspiration from her brow.

"Because you're a damn good man to have between the sheets."

He shook with silent laughter. "You wouldn't have lasted in Eden as long as poor Eve, my Shay."

"Aren't you glad?"

"If you're asking if I love you, the answer is yes." He pressed a soft kiss onto her mouth. "And don't ever change. I love you just as you are."

More
Sandra Brown!

Please turn this page
for a
bonus excerpt
from

LOVE'S ENCORE

available
wherever books are sold.

Camille brought her compact car to an abrupt stop as she caught her first glimpse of Bridal Wreath. She had followed the directions given her at the tourist information office in historic Stanton Hall and taken Homochitto Street from downtown Natchez. The lady behind the desk told her that the lane leading to the old mansion would be on her left just before the road she was on intersected with Highway 65.

She almost missed the small, weather-faded sign obscured by thick shrubbery designating that this unpaved trail was the driveway she sought. She wended her way over the deep potholes while marveling at the enormous oaks trailing their gray, beardlike moss from branches of inestimable proportions; the magnolias that still retained a few creamy, fragrant, white blossoms, despite the lateness of the season; and the fountainlike formation of the shrubs lining the drive that had given the plantation house its name. The snowy flowers of the bridal wreath had long since disappeared in the summer's heat, but the branches were thick with their dainty, bright green foliage.

Camille opened the car door and stepped out, leaving the engine to idle. She gazed at the house before her. The basic facts of its history flashed through her mind. It had been built in 1805. The colonial architecture depicted the period. It had two stories. The rooms on the second floor opened onto a balcony that provided a roof for the front porch surrounding the first floor on three sides. The structure was red brick, though the years had faded the color to a dull rose. Six white columns rose majestically from the porch to support the balcony. Tall, wide windows flanked by forest green shutters were symmetrically spaced, three on each side of the huge front door, which was white. Suspended on a heavy chain was a brass chandelier hanging just over the front door.

Camille Jameson sighed in ecstasy and climbed back into her car. As she engaged the gears she laughed out loud and shouted, "Scarlett O'Hara, eat your heart out!"

That she had been hired to restore this mansion to its former glory was an intoxicating thought. She prayed silently that she would be able to meet the challenge. It was important to her career as a decorator and to her financial future.

Camille and her mother, Martha, owned a decorating business in Atlanta. Martha Jameson had tried to maintain it after Camille's father died, but by the time Camille had graduated from college with her decorator's degree, it had deteriorated into little more than a gift shop featuring undistinguished antiques and mediocre bric-a-brac. Camille soon began ordering contemporary decorating items and increasing the quality of the antiques they stocked. She offered her services as a consultant to customers who sought advice in their choice of wallpaper, carpet, draperies, furniture, and entire decorating schemes. Camille's good taste and easy, friendly manner had soon earned her a reputation and a respectable clientele. She now employed two other women who helped in the "studio," while her mother handled over-the-counter sales and the bookkeeping.

When Camille had been approached by Mr. Rayburn Prescott of Natchez, Mississippi, to redo his mansion, she jumped at the chance. This was by far her most important commission. She was well acquainted with the antebellum homes of old Natchez. She and her mother had toured the restored houses during one of the annual spring pilgrimages. Camille had been a young girl then, but those lovely homes had made a lasting impression on her.

Rayburn Prescott was the typical Southern gentleman, using courtly manners when addressing Camille or Martha. The other ladies in the studio had twittered when he spoke to them in a drawl more pronounced than they were accustomed to hearing even in Atlanta. His shock of white hair was still thick and waved away from a broad, high forehead. His blue eyes retained a sparkle, though he must have been approaching seventy. He was tall, stately, distinguished, and eloquent.

After the preliminaries of getting acquainted, he told Camille about his house in Natchez. "I'm ashamed of it, Miss Jameson. After my wife died, over twenty years ago, I let it fall into a sad state of disrepair. It has become a bachelor's house. My son spends most of his waking hours at our plantation across the river, but he agrees with me that we should restore Bridal Wreath to its original beauty."

"It has such a lovely name," Camille mused, already conjuring up pictures of the house in her mind. "I'll gladly accept your commission."

"But we haven't even talked about your fee or any of the details!" he exclaimed.

"It doesn't matter. I know I want to do it." She laughed at his surprised expression before his face crinkled into a pleasant smile. She had come highly recommended by a friend of his who owned a restaurant in Peachtree Plaza that Camille had decorated. Rayburn Prescott was convinced of her abilities. They talked about her fee and she was astounded at the sum he quoted. He gave her an almost limitless budget for the restoration. Apparently she wouldn't have to consciously economize. He insisted that she stay at Bridal Wreath during the restoration, promising that arrangements to that effect would be made for her. They set a mutually convenient date for her arrival, and now she was here, standing on the front porch, her purse under her arm, waiting for the bell she had rung to be answered. Upon close inspection, she noticed the chipping paint, the dulling rust that was corroding the brass appointments on the front door, and the warped boards waving the front porch beneath her feet. If the interior were as bad as the exterior, she had a lot of work to do.

Camille smiled wryly to herself. Work was *all* she had to do. Her life revolved around her career, much to the consternation of her mother and close friends, most of whom had husbands and several children. Her mother encouraged her to date the young men who stopped by the studio on contrived business, but Camille remained aloof to their advances. She passed off their flirtations as inconsequential, and Martha Jameson worried about her daughter's obvious lack of interest in the opposite sex.

It distressed Camille to see her mother so frustrated over her love life, or rather the lack of one, but she couldn't tell her the reason. She couldn't say, "Mother, I gave myself to a man once, and all I felt afterward was shame and humiliation. I don't intend to fall into that trap again." One didn't tell one's mother things like that. Besides, some memories were too painful to articulate. Camille shuddered and drew a long sigh at these recollections just as the front door opened. She looked into a smiling face.

"Hello. I'm Camille Jameson." She smiled, not knowing how fetching she looked with the sunlight bouncing off her dark, curly hair.

"Hello, Miss Jameson." The man's welcoming face was wreathed in smiles. "Mr. Prescott is waiting for you. He's as excited as a schoolboy going to his first dance. I'm sure glad you made the trip safely. He's been worried about a young lady like you driving herself all the way from Atlanta."

"I had no trouble on the trip, and I'm just as anxious to see Mr. Prescott again." She stepped into the entrance hall as the man moved aside. She glanced around her in awe. It was just as she hoped it would be!

"My name is Simon Mitchell, Miss Jameson. Anytime you need anything, you call on me," the man said, drawing her attention momentarily away from her perusal of the house.

"Thank you, Mr. Mitchell." Her smile was genuine.

"Simon, please. Have a seat, Miss Jameson, and I'll go find Mr. Prescott. I think he's out back watering his plants."

"Take your time. I won't mind waiting." He nodded and moved toward the back of the house down the broad hall that ran its length. Camille longed to peer into the rooms that opened off the corridor, but felt she should wait for her host and new employer to show her through his home. Southerners like Rayburn Prescott were scrupulous about manners and etiquette.

She sat down on a chair in the hall and assumed the ladylike pose drilled into her by her mother: back straight, knees together, hands reposing gracefully in her lap. She suddenly wished she had a more refined look. She was cursed with dark, curly hair that she wore at a medium length so that on particularly humid days, she could pull it back into a chignon when only the tendrils around her face escaped into unruly curls. The dark hair was complemented by her apricot-toned skin. It wasn't dark enough to be called olive, and not rosy enough to be fair. Instead it glowed with the color of warm honey. She had always coveted her friends who had Dresden complexions that blushed becomingly. She saw no compensation in having skin that tanned to a dusky hue under the summer sun. And no one else on earth had eyes like hers. Why couldn't she have plain blue or green or hazel or even brown without those silly golden highlights in them? Other brown eyes were touched with a spark of hazel, or were mysteriously deep like ebony, but hers reflected gold in their depths. She hated them. Her long, dark lashes, wide, generous mouth, and pert nose had combined with her hair to give her a gypsy look. That had been her father's pet name for her—his little gypsy.

She couldn't help her features, so she saw to it that she was always dressed with utmost care. Her flair for color and design, which was so valuable to her vocation, went into her wardrobe, too. Now, she tugged the skirt of her yellow linen suit over her knees, wishing she might take off the jacket and wear only the cool, sheer print voile blouse underneath. The humidity in Natchez was wilting her clothes, not to mention what it was doing to her hair, which she had tamed into a semblance of control this morning. Now she knew it must be curling around her head in wild abandon.

She heard the crunch of tires on the driveway outside and then the loudly squeaking sound of a car door being slammed shut. She counted the three steps that she remembered leading up to the porch as someone took them quickly and then three more long steps across the front porch to the door. The knob on the door turned and it was flung open. It swung back and crashed into the wall before the looming figure standing silhouetted against the afternoon sun reached behind himself to close it. He stamped into the entrance hall, leaving muddy scuff marks on the parquet oak floor. He moved with an easy gait that was vaguely familiar, but Camille was so infuriated with his negligent disregard for the abused floor, the door, and the wall, that she didn't give the familiarity a conscious thought. Before she reasoned against speaking out, she blurted, "It's no wonder this house is in such deplorable shape. If everyone who came in here was as careless as you are and as unappreciative of its beauty, it would be falling down within a week!"

The man stopped suddenly and glanced quickly around the hall, surprised by the feminine voice that was berating him. He had just come in from the blindingly bright sunlight, and it took a moment for him to adjust his eyes and spot her sitting in the shadows of the hallway. Without speaking, he removed his wide-brimmed straw hat and raked his arm across a perspiring forehead. Then, still holding his hat in one hand, he put both hands on his hips and looked at her fully for the first time.

"I beg your pardon," he said with deceptive calm, anger just below the surface. He took five steps forward and stopped within a few feet of her chair. Their gazes met and locked and there was a simultaneous sharp intake of breath from the two people staring at each other.

It couldn't be! He couldn't be here! What was he doing here? Is it him? Yes! No! It can't be! Camille's mouth had gone as dry as cotton and she tried convulsively to swallow. Her heart was pounding so hard she knew he must be able to see it stirring the fabric across her breasts. She flushed hot all over and then shivered with cold. The roaring in her ears was like a cannon blast. She knew by his stance and shocked expression that he was as dumbstruck as she.

He looked the same as he had in Utah almost two years ago. Maybe there were a few more weblike lines fanning out from the corners of his eyes, but the irises were as blue as ever, startling, piercing, hypnotizing. She knew all too well their hypnotic power! Was he taller? No. It must seem so because she was sitting down, but she knew that if she stood, she would still only reach his collarbone. He was as broad of shoulder and narrow of hip as she remembered. The physique that had been a part of her fantasies for these many months had not been exaggerated in her memory as she sometimes convinced herself that it was. His brown hair was streaked with sun-bleached strands. The tan skin drawn tightly over the lean lines of his face intensified the blue of his eyes, which studied her with the same hungry stare she felt in her own.

He wasn't dressed in the tight ski pants and soft sweaters she remembered. He wore western-cut jeans and cowboy boots—muddy boots that scuffed up floors. His blue chambray shirt was unbuttoned to the middle of his chest, the sleeves rolled to his elbows. It was damp and stained with perspiration. The hair on his arms and chest was bleached almost completely blond, and nestled in the curls on his chest was the gold ornament that Camille remembered tenderly. He told her the cross had belonged to his late mother. The chain that suspended it around his neck was heavy. In no way did the piece of jewelry look feminine, especially lying as it was in the damp hair of his chest.

"Zack Prescott?" She was barely able to verbalize his name. When Mr. Rayburn Prescott had introduced himself to her, said his name, she felt that sharp pang around her heart that accompanied any reminder of the skiing vacation she had taken after her graduation from college. She would never have imagined that those two men would be related. Zack had never told her where he called home. Had she ever asked? Had she cared?

"Don't I know you from somewhere?" He parroted the corny Hollywood line with all the sarcasm he could muster.

The tightness in Camille's throat relaxed long enough for her to say, "You told me you were a farmer, but I assumed you were joking." She tried to smile but her lips were quivering. The muscles of her face wouldn't work.

The lines on either side of his mouth hardened. "What else did you 'assume' about me? I'd be curious to know."

The bitterness underlying his words stung Camille, and she flinched. Then the familiar regrets that had haunted her for days, months, years came back and with them the guilt and shame he had caused her to suffer. Anger flared from the golden depths of her eyes as she snarled, "What do you think I assumed about a man who so heartlessly seduced an innocent girl."

"No less than he assumed about a *woman* so easily seduced." His words fell on her like physical blows and she catapulted out of the chair to stand directly in front of him.

"You . . . you're hateful and immoral, without conscience. I despise you for what you did to me—"

"You have an unconvincing way of displaying your aversion, Camille," he interrupted her, and she wanted to slap his arrogant face. But the sound of her name coming from those full, soft, sensual lips halted any action she would have taken. She had the overwhelming compulsion to reach out and stroke his lean, brown cheek. She clenched her fists to stymie the impulse. They stared at each other for a long moment before they heard Simon's footsteps coming down the hall. Camille whirled away from Zack and tried vainly to compose her features.

"Miss Jameson, Mr. Prescott will see you now. Hello,

Zack. Have you met Miss Jameson?" Camille had her back to him, and Zack must have nodded in acknowledgment, for he didn't speak. "Well then, you come with me, Miss Jameson, and Zack can join you for refreshments later. Mr. Prescott hopes you don't mind meeting him on the terrace."

"N-no, that's fine." Anything to get away from the disturbing presence behind her. She followed Simon down the hall without looking back.

To read more, look for *Love's Encore*
by Sandra Brown.

SANDRA BROWN is the author of over sixty books, of which over fifty were *New York Times* bestsellers, including the #1 *New York Times* bestseller *The Alibi, The Crush, Envy, The Switch, Standoff, Unspeakable, Fat Tuesday, Exclusive, The Witness, Charade, Where There's Smoke,* and *French Silk.* Her novels have been published in more than thirty languages. She and her husband live in Texas.